BOBO'S RAID

by

Mike Downs

ISBN 978-1489575296
Copyright 2013 Mike Downs
all rights reserved

Books by Mike Downs

The Artimus Box

Novac's Race

Novac's Run

Bobo's Raid

Author's Note

Please keep in mind that this is a work of fiction. The names, characters, organizations, dates, and events in this novel are a product of the author's imagination, or are used fictitiously. Any resemblance to actual events or persons living or dead is purely coincidental.

This book is available in print and digital formats at most online retailers.

Acknowledgements

A special thanks to Kathy Downs for the cover art and editing.

Thank you to Peggy and Kas Kastner, Phyllis Gurney, and Eileen Adams for their encouragement, and for reading the drafts and making useful suggestions.

And finally thank you to The San Francisco Maritime Library for their help with the shipping details.

For Halftrack

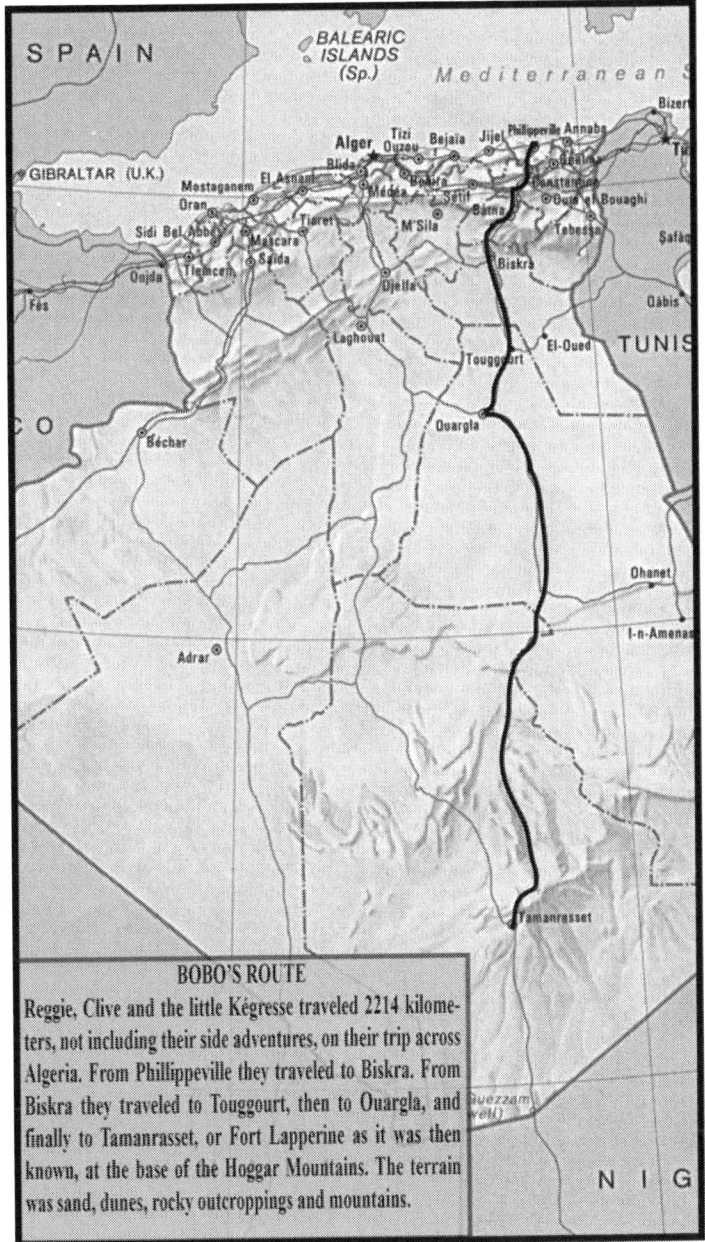

BOBO'S ROUTE

Reggie, Clive and the little Kégresse traveled 2214 kilometers, not including their side adventures, on their trip across Algeria. From Phillippeville they traveled to Biskra. From Biskra they traveled to Touggourt, then to Ouargla, and finally to Tamanrasset, or Fort Lapperine as it was then known, at the base of the Hoggar Mountains. The terrain was sand, dunes, rocky outcroppings and mountains.

Prologue

In the winter of 1922 two great French adventurers, Georges-Marie Haardt and Louis Audoin-Dubreuil, set out to conquer the Sahara in Citroën Kégresse half-tracked vehicles. André Citroën had dreamed up the idea to promote his company. The "Cruise," or "Raid," was to go south from Touggourt, Algeria to Timbuktu, Sudan in 20 days.

With supreme reliability, the incredible Citroëns made easy work of the trip. Two years later the same two men crossed Africa to the Indian Ocean and on to Madagascar by ferry.

In 1931 Haardt and Audoin teamed up again to take the Citroën Kégresses from Beirut to Beijing. They would travel 30,000 kilometers. The trip took them over the Himalayas in a truly herculean endeavor. However Haardt, utterly exhausted by the grind, died in Hong Kong. The little caterpillar trucks were a great success: loved by their drivers and revered by all who witnessed their journeys.

This novel brings into play once again, the great "little caterpillar" as the French fondly referred to the Citroën.

Mike Downs

Pendine Sands, Wales 1928

Count Reginald Bobrowski uses the chamois sewed to the back of his sleeve to clear the salt spray from his goggles. The weather is unsettled and overcast under a threatening slate-gray sky. A cold sea broods with snarling waves that pound angrily at the beach, clawing away at the sand. The narrow strip of sand left is getting too soft for a record run. Disregarding the beach's condition, the Count hurtles down the diminishing pathway in his huge ponderous beast at almost 130 miles an hour.

The car is his own creation. The sheer size of the car is closer to a locomotive than an automobile. He and his friend, Clive Parry-Jones, have spent months building the beast at the Count's large country estate. They took the engine from a World War I fighter plane. The 27 liters of thundering horsepower make the engine cover look impossibly long from the cockpit.

The individual exhaust pipes protruding from the sides of the engine are each the size of a man's leg. They lead to sewer-sized pipes running down both sides of the car to end behind the rear wheels. Enormous wheels with narrow tires are almost the height of the radiator. Big chain sprockets that drive the rear wheels are just forward of the cockpit at axle level. The cowl of the car is so high the Count has to lean to the right to see ahead.

The soft sand makes it difficult to keep the car straight; as the car hits another soft spot it bounces into the air. When it returns to earth, the rear wheels spin causing the car to yaw sideways. Count Bobrowski fights the giant steering wheel, his head bobbing with the bumps.

He momentarily lifts the throttle to correct the car's path. To set a record, lifting the throttle is the last thing he wants to do. Reggie slams his foot back down hard on the gas pedal, the engine screams, then suddenly runs wild. The large-linked drive chain snaps. Freed from the sprockets, the broken chain rips the cap and goggles from Reggie's head, then flies across the sand like a demented snake. The car slews to a stop and the dazed pilot slowly climbs from the cockpit. With its wheels now settling deep in the wet sand, the wounded behemoth spits and belches steam from the radiator as if in protest.

Reggie is a tall slender man. His slicked-back black hair and pencil thin mustache lend him that suave Valentino look. He staggers a few paces from the car and sits heavily on a dry lump of sand. The Count puts his hand to his head; the touch stings and his gloved hand comes away scarlet with blood.

He flicks the blood from his eye to see a figure running down the beach toward him. As the figure grows closer, Reggie sees his old friend Clive Parry-Jones. The man's face is red as a beet. His light-complexioned freckled face is pure English. He is a bit portly and puffing hard, fighting for air. When he reaches the Count, he stops, hunching over with his hands on his knees, gulping air.

BOBO'S RAID

He hands Reggie a handkerchief and studies the Count's face with some concern. "Are you all right?" he pants.

"I seem to be in better shape than those standing before me, old man," replies the Count. "Sit down Jonesy, you're making me dizzy. Have you got a fag? I didn't bring mine."

Parry-Jones shakes out a cigarette from a crumpled pack in his pocket and gives it to the Count.

"So, Bobo old man, what happened to the car?"

"The old girl threw her chain again. I hit some loose sand and lifted. I jumped back on the throttle too hard and snapped the bloody chain. We need to update the drive on her. And for the millionth time, stop calling me that. I really must tell Ally to stop. It seemed a grand old lark before we were married, but I no longer find the "Bobo" moniker amusing."

"Good luck on that Reggie. I cannot remember the last time Ally took instruction from you."

"Too right old man. I suppose I should leave it, but that is no reason for you to go on with it."

"Okay, okay, what do you want to do now?"

"Let's pack it in. Ally wants to see the sands of the Sahara. I think it's time to change direction. I want to enter the race at Indianapolis anyway. The Bugatti boys think they have a car to claim some of that fantastic prize money. Going to America, and doing some races at Brooklands will take up most of our time. So I think we'll take the car home and make it into a desert roamer. I've had enough of her trying to rip my head off. We'll put a big touring body on her and pack it with all we'll need to drive on the sands in some degree of comfort. You can bring your bride, Fay, and we can lie about swilling champagne and munch on pickled herring, or the like."

"Jolly good, Reggie. We should get back to the ladies if we want to have any hope of peace tonight."

"Yeah, jolly good. You know Jonesy, I spent most of my youth in America. The 'jolly goods' and 'old mans' are just not a natural way of speaking for me."

"That's all right old son. Most of us try to overlook your heathen upbringing in the backwoods of the colonies."

"Wow, that's really gracious of you, my most learned English friend. Let's go."

Alexandra, the Count's wife, is a stunning strawberry blonde. She comes from a well-to-do American family that encouraged her independent spirit. She is not the typical slender, bobbed-hair flapper that is popular with her American friends. Her hourglass figure and fair skin allude to a sweet innocence. Her hair shines with sunlight and falls gently to below her shoulders.

The Count loves to recount the story of their first meeting. He was late to a meeting in her father's bank and hurrying to an elevator when he first saw her. He could not tear his eyes away from her and failed to notice the elevator doors were closing. He smacked his head on the door and staggered backwards. Ally says she loved the way he laughed at his own embarrassment while he was rubbing his bruised forehead.

She insists on Jonesy driving them back to their country estate near Reading. They leave the beast in Pendine to have it hauled back later. Reggie rides in the back of the Rolls Royce, with Ally attending to the lacerations on his head. He rests his head on her lap with her soft hands caressing his face, then drifts off to sleep.

When Reggie wakes from his nap, his first thought is the lost cap. "Ally, did anyone find my cap?"

"No, and I for one am glad it is gone. You wear the most outlandish hats my dear."

"A Florida golfer's cap is all the rage. I thought I looked quite dashing; it is becoming somewhat of a trademark."

"I am grateful that the silly thing kept my handsome Bobo's head intact. We are becoming known for your colorful attire."

Reggie nods at what he perceives is a compliment. "We are quite the trendsetters all right. Let's stop for lunch, Jonesy. There's a good little pub up ahead."

The two wives sit across from each other quietly chatting. The men, after finishing their lunch, are brandishing pencils and scribbling new car designs on bits of paper. The Count, chewing on the end of his pencil, studies the latest scrawls.

"We need a new rear axle and driveshaft; maybe we should fit the car with dual rear wheels. I don't think we want an open car for driving in the desert. I'll call the coach builder and see about sealing the doors and windows to keep the sand out. We can spray it with white paint to keep it cool in the sun, too."

Alexandra and Fay stop chatting and almost in the same breath say, "Make sure we have plenty of room for our luggage." Reggie and Jonesy both roll their eyes.

The rest of 1928 goes by with races at Brooklands and a grand trip to America to race the Bugatti in the Indianapolis 500. The Count makes a fine start, climbing through the field only to have the engine explode into ruin with connecting rod failure. After the race, he and Ally catch up with their American friends on what is known as a booze cruise on the east coast. Luxury liners are doing a brisk business during prohibition serving liquor to thirsty Americans while out to sea.

When they return to England, and after much modification to the beast's chassis, the two men take the car to the coachbuilder's shop. The coachbuilder takes the next year to finish the new four-door body. It is early 1930 by the time the foursome are ready to tackle the rigors of Algeria.

The trip comes with adventure and hardship. The car overheats constantly except during the frigid nights and in the icy mountain passes. Sharp stones puncture the tires. The lever action shock absorbers leak their fluids making for a bone-crushing ride over bumps.

They find the native Berbers to be friendly and helpful. They own little, scraping by farming crops from an unforgiving land and raising sheep. On some of the most barren stretches, the people invite them into their mud hut homes to drink mint tea. The Berbers' willingness to share what they have gives pause to the Count's troupe. They think of the riches they enjoy in the cool English climate. Ally and Fay insist on buying colorful rugs and cloaks woven by the Berber women. The Berber generosity, however unexpected, is a welcome excuse to get out of the jouncing car and stifling heat.

Coming through a snow-covered mountain pass into a valley, a huge sand storm blots out the sun. The sand blows through the valley floor funneled by the high walls. The swirling cloud is so thick it is as if a curtain dropped killing any light.

For two days, the couples sit out the whistling sands in the car. When the storm first hit, the couples thought of it as another part of their grand adventure. The intensity of the wind would rise and fall. Sleeping in the car was not at all comfortable: the shrieking of the wind and blasts of sand made for a fitful night.

Sand clogged the vents the men had built in the roof and back of the car. Breathing became labored, but when Reggie and Clive pulled the gauze filtering material from the vents the car soon filled with dust and silt.

When relieving themselves became an absolute necessity the unfortunate would quickly duck out the door. Returning would bring an unbelievable rise in volume of the banshee wind, a huge deposit of sand, and the unfortunate almost as miserable as when he exited.

By the next day every surface inside the car was covered with sand. No one was telling silly stories anymore to keep up moral. With the heat rising in the car, and sand in their hair and clothing, it was just not fun anymore.

When the shrieking howl of the wind finally stopped, it was not a period of tapering off, but an abrupt end. From having to scream to be heard suddenly all was eerily still. Reggie cautiously opened a door, sure that the terrible wind would return. The landscape was clear and bright, the sky a cloudless brilliant blue. It was as if the sand storm had been a dream, or rather a nightmare. The women waited while Clive setup a portable shower. With their hair still wet, the women set about cleaning out the sand out of the car.

Clive and Reggie took their turns in the shower. There was just enough trickle of water to wash off most of the sand. Each of them commented that it took days to get all of the sand out of their ears and teeth. A meal of canned meat and biscuits brought back most of the good humor lost in the storm. Reggie, after inspecting his creation, shook his head and laughed; the sand blasted away spots of the white paint from the car. He told Jonesy he was going to rename the car Guernsey.

When finally getting underway again the car traveled less than 100 yards and chugged to a stop. In their haste to get moving, both men forgot about the carburetor air cleaner. Sand again was everywhere. Jonesy found the air cleaner completely clogged with it. After cleaning out the filter and changing the spark plugs, they were off again. The long trip, with the breakdowns and stops, wore the group out.

After reaching the flat lands, Reggie feels that he has fulfilled his promise to Ally to drive on the sands of the Sahara. When he asks if all agree their response is immediate. They have seen enough. Ally and Fay say, "Let's go home!" in unison. Everyone is anxious to feel the coolness and see the green fields of England. Not to mention the comforts all of them groaned about missing while they waited out the sand storm in the confines of the car.

Chapter 2

After returning to England, Reggie's business interest turns to railroads. He has a narrow gauge track laid out around his estate and purchases an engine and several cars to examine how they work. After some commercial studies, he decides to expand and spends several years laying tracks to increase commerce between the neighboring towns.

Lord Chaddick, a large landowner, invites Reggie and Ally to a party he is giving to celebrate the completion of the railway through his properties. They arrive at the sprawling old country manor, and after the butler takes their coats and hats, Lord Chaddick greets them. He pumps the Count's hand and bows to kiss Ally's hand.

"Welcome, welcome, so nice of you to come. Let me get you a drink, Count. I will introduce the Countess to the women. By the by, I have a man in the library I would like you to meet."

Lord Chaddick ushers Ally into the huge main room teeming with men and women in fancy dress. He guides the Countess to a group of women and introduces her to a large, heavily-rouged woman.

"You will be in the best of hands with Lady Chaddick, Countess. I must be off to get your husband his drink."

The Lord returns to Reggie with a large glass of whisky and takes him by the arm to lead him to the library, entering the room through an ornately carved wooden door. The room, richly paneled with a beautiful wood, smells of pipe tobacco. Leather-bound books fill the shelves all the way to the ceiling. Views of the splendid gardens and pastoral grounds are visible through the windows.

A man with a bushy mustache sits behind a surprisingly modern art deco desk. Smoking a cigar, and holding a glass of amber liquid, the man seems to be in relaxed possession of the room.

"Count," Lord Chaddick says, "let me introduce you to Sir Benton Smyth."

Reggie starts forward to shake the man's hand.

"Please be seated, Count," says the man behind the desk. He remains seated, and makes no move to shake hands. "Lord Chaddick, this is a matter of some delicacy; you won't mind leaving us to it, will you old man?"

Lord Chaddick, without a word, meekly withdraws from the room.

"I am simply known as S or Mr. S. This, by tradition, denotes me as the head of my organization. I wish to speak with you about your trip to Algeria."

"My trip there was over three years ago, Mr. S. What would you like to know sir?"

Mr. S puffs his cigar, blows a plume of smoke into the air and says, "I am curious to know why you went to Algeria. We do not seem to have much information on what sort of business you were involved in there. Do you do anything of substance with your life, Count? From what I see you skate along as if life for you were a simple lark. England needs stout fellows now. The situation in Europe is grave. The days of rich playboys larking about are over."

Reggie, somewhat taken aback, answers, "Are you always this rude? I can tell you I took my wife and friends for an outing to see the sands of the Sahara. There was no more to it than that. As to your question of what I may do with my life, that would be my business. Excuse me S, I need some fresh air."

Mr. S rises from his chair, snarling, "Don't turn your back to me, you little popinjay. You will stand and deliver a complete report of the route you took through Algeria before you leave this room." Mr. S, thumping the desk with his fist, his face flushed, yells, "You will not leave this room until I am finished with you."

Reggie gives a jaunty wave as he closes the door behind him. Walking into the room full of guests he sees Ally with a small group of women. Ally sees him coming and breaks away from the group.

"You look angry, Bobo. What is the trouble?"

"Lord Chaddick had a surprise guest waiting to attack me in his library. A man that calls himself Mr. S. The guy's a jerk. I'm going to say hello to a few people here and then we are going to leave. We'll go into town and have some dinner. It'll be nice to spend some time alone with you. We never seem to have time to just sit and chat by ourselves anymore."

Ally takes his hand and looks at him with concern. "How did he attack you? Are you all right?"

Reggie takes a flute of champagne off a tray. Before taking a sip, he says, "I shouldn't have said attacked. I meant verbally. The guy's some kind of government johnny, you know, all king and country fall on my sword type. One of the betters, meaning he thinks he's better than anyone else."

Ally smiles and gives his hand a little squeeze. "I'd say he made quite an impression."

The next morning Reggie wakes to a tapping on his bedroom door. His clearly agitated butler says that the police are in the foyer. "They want to see you sir. They say they have orders to take you to London."

"Take me to London? What the hell for? Oh never mind, please tell them to wait while I get dressed." He throws back the covers and heads for the bathroom.

Ally, propped up on her elbow, smiles watching the Count as he stretches and scratches his backside.

"What have you done now, Bobo? Do the police take you to London for speeding tickets?"

Reggie turns and says, "No, not for speeding tickets. I think this has something to do with my friend Mr. S. Let me get washed up; we'll talk before I go."

Reggie finishes shaving and comes into the bedroom to dress.

"Ally, I want you to call our lawyer and put him on alert. If this is something to do with Mr.S, I'll probably need him. I'll call you as soon as I know what's going on."

Reggie dresses and Ally helps him with his tie. He gives her a kiss and says, "Don't worry, love, I'll be back soon."

The men waiting for Reggie are not local police, and are in a hurry to get him into their car. The Count asks them for identification which seems to exasperate the two men. After each man shows him a Special Branch card, he asks why the trip to London.

BOBO'S RAID

"We are under orders to take you to a meeting with S; we are not permitted to elaborate sir. If you are ready, we need to get going."

The men descend the front steps of the house and get into a Humber Pullman 4-door sedan. The Count sits in the back along with one of the Special Branch men. The forty-mile trip goes by without further conversation.

After dodging in and out of the busy London traffic, the car stops at a warehouse on the Thames River. The driver gets out of the Humber and opens the door for Reggie. The three men walk through the front doors of the warehouse into a small foyer. On the far side of the foyer are two armed guards standing beside the double doors that are the main entrance.

One of the guards steps forward to inspect credentials before letting the men pass through. The floor of the warehouse contains stacks of wooden crates. To the left are stairs leading to two upper levels of offices. After they climb to the top level, the men put Reggie in a windowless room and lock the door behind them.

An hour passes. The room that smells of stale tobacco becomes unpleasantly hot. Reggie notes there is an open grate on a wall pouring in heated air. Reggie crosses the room to the door and pounds on it.

"All right, I am sufficiently impressed Mr. S, can we get on with it now?" He returns to a chair and waits another twenty minutes before Mr. S enters the room with the two men who brought Reggie from Reading.

S puts a file folder down on a table. He instructs the Special Branch men to stand by the open door. He sits by the table and opens the file. "Are you ready to resume our chat, Count?"

Reggie, wiping his brow with a handkerchief, says, "What is it that you want, S? Am I to be impressed with your ability to abduct me?"

S fidgets with the ends of his mustache, "You should appreciate that I can have you taken at any time it suits me. I find your attitude lacking. This is a matter of British security. You will answer my questions as I put them to you. Do you understand me?"

Reggie settles back in his chair and lights a cigarette. "You have my attention, sir."

S puts on reading glasses and says, "I want to know the route you took through Algeria, for a start."

"We started in Algiers and traveled east and then south to Biskra. From there we continued south to Tuoggourt and on to just outside of Ouargla."

S is tracing the route with his finger on the map he spread out on the table. "Ouargla was as far south as you went?"

"Yes," Reggie replies.

S looks up from the map. "You did not make it very far. Was the trip too strenuous for you?"

"We had a great deal of trouble with the car, and the heat and sand storms were taking the fun out of it. So yes would be the answer to that."

S shakes his head to show his displeasure. "Did you meet any Germans on your little soirée?"

"I don't recall any, most of the people were French or Berber. Look, we cleared our passports with the proper authorities before we left. What is it you want?"

S brushes ash from his jacket. "I do not like your kind, Bobrowski. What I want is for you to take a trip for us back to Algeria and keep an eye on the Jerrys. We know they are looking for oil and if they find any we want to know where. You will have to be able to travel much farther south than your little band of merrymakers did before.

"We are going to give you a course in oil geology; you could be in country for six to eight months. You will report to us by radio. I want all of you to learn the operation of transmitting and receiving."

Reggie sits up in his chair. "What do you mean all of us?"

"I want your wife and your friends to go with you, the same as your last trip."

"You're nuts, my dear Mr. S. That's not going to happen. I will not put my wife or Clive's in that sort of situation. If you need spies you are going to have to find them from one of your own services."

S pounds his fist on the table. "Never take that tone with me. You will do exactly as I say. I can have Inland Revenue go through your estate taxes as well as your mother's. I will have them impound all of your properties in Britain. I can have your mother arrested, and all of her interests investigated. You will be years giving evidence. I will keep you tied up with legalities and your mother in prison for as long as it takes to get though the system.

"From the files we have, I see you were born in Poland, and spent much of your childhood in America. Your mother is American as is your wife. The property and holdings your family has in England are extensive. Your mother has an interesting manner of dodging taxation here."

"You're a right bastard, S. I'll have my attorneys on you. You will not get away with this."

"Your attorneys, as you call them, will have no effect. You are not dealing with civil authority. I represent the British government in this matter. This operation has approval from the highest authority."

"You can try your worst, S. I will not subject my wife to any danger in that miserable desert; there is no authority on this earth that can make me. If you insist on this madness, I could go. Clive can choose to go or not, but his wife will not go either. I don't think you have any idea of who you are fooling with if you think you're going to take a run at my mother. I can guarantee she will chew you up and spit you out."

S smiles through his mustache, "If you agree to Algeria it may not be necessary to find who can swing the larger axe. When can you be ready to leave?"

"In a year, perhaps, if I can equip by then."

S begins to flush, "A year will not do. You need to be in country within weeks."

Reggie's head jerks back, his eyes wide with disbelief. "That's out of the question. If I'm not equipped properly, I will have no chance of following your Jerrys around. I will need a vehicle that can travel the desert sand dunes and mountain passes without breakdowns. I have in mind a half-track truck that can carry spares and all the equipment we'll need to survive."

"What do you mean?" says S. "We can provide a suitable car and you make do with it."

"No, that's not on," counters Reggie. "I'm not going to put Clive or myself at the mercy of the desert again. We were lucky to make it out of there last time.

It would do you no good to lose us out there. We can't report the movements of the Jerrys if we can't follow them.

"I thought of designing a vehicle to traverse the sands and be fast on hard surfaces. I can't see getting it built and tested in under a year. If you are in such a hurry though, I have another idea. The Polish army just took delivery of the newest Citroën Kégresse half-track vehicles. Let me see if I can arrange for you to buy one. Clive and I can modify it to do the job and we can be off."

S rises from his chair sputtering, "If you need this Citroën thing you can buy it. England has given you a home and a place to extend your wealth. You owe this country. You will not make any demands on England or my department. This is a way that you can pay back this country for your dallying. I can and will make your life a misery. I can make the wealth you have disappear. Do I make myself clear?

"Okay S. You know, I can go to the Sahara and do your spying as an adventure, but that's the only way I'm going. Your stupid threats are falling on deaf ears. You can pay for the vehicle, and I'll pay for the equipment and the trip's expenses. On the other hand, you can pay for the equipment and trip expenses if you prefer. I have the contacts necessary in Poland to secure the vehicle. If you will be so kind as to return me to my home, I'll get to work on it."

"I want a daily report from you Count. We will meet again in a week, and by that time, I will expect a date of departure. I will be sending one or two of my people with you on the trip."

"I'll need to know how many people you want to come S; it will make a big difference in space and provisions. I'll see you next week...and I can drive myself here."

Reggie turns and walks to the door, the guard opens the door for him and S, unwilling to let him have the last word, says, "You are an insolent bugger, but you will come to heel."

"Huff and puff," Reggie says as he goes through the door.

Chapter 3

On returning home, he explains his meeting with S to Ally. She is not pleased that her Bobo has to go on a wild goose chase for S, and more so when he tells her it is men only. She will not be able to share in the adventure.

"I can call my father," she says.

"No my dear. As much as I dislike the man, S may have a point. Germany is a threat, war could break out anytime now. I have never done service for England or Poland for that matter. We live here and I should do my part. I don't see much trouble in this trip; if we stay smart we'll keep our necks. I will miss you most of all. That will probably the hardest thing to overcome."

"We can go home to America, Reggie. We don't have to live here."

"No, Ally, that would be like running away. I can't do that. This will be fun anyway. I'll get one of the Polish army's new Citroëns; we can go anywhere with it."

"Bobo, just think of all the problems we had and we didn't get very far into the desert."

"What happened to Reggie? I thought for a minute we were over the Bobo tag. I do wish you didn't call me that, everyone is making fun of me."

"Oh no dear, Bobo is my special name for you. But I will try not to use it in front of other people if that will make you happy. I am still worried about you traveling in that blasted desert though."

"I don't want you to worry Ally; I found an article in an old magazine for you. It's all about the Citroën Kégresses that drove from Touggourt to Timbuktu in 20 days. By the way, a couple of years ago, Citroën sent the trucks from Beirut to Beijing. They have half-tracks like tanks or tractors except the tracks are made of rubber. They go up mountains in the snow, and one pulled a huge motor home up a 350-foot sand dune. The desert does not present a problem for these things. They seem to be as reliable as a train, too."

"How long will you be gone?"

"It should be a few months. We'll have a radio with us and I'll get one installed here so we can talk. You'll have to learn how to use it, but that won't give you any trouble. I really don't want to leave you alone too long Ally. You're just too damn beautiful to be left alone for long."

"I hope you're trying to be sweet Reggie, but there is no one for me but you. You do know that, don't you?"

"I know, Ally, but I still think of it sometimes. Anyway have a look at the magazine dear. I have to call Jonesy and get the ball rolling on this thing. Oh, by the way, S wants me to report to him every day, so he may call or send his troops when I don't report. He'll have to get used to it though. I have no intention of making daily reports."

Reggie calls Clive Parry-Jones and they are soon together in the estate's workshop going over plans.

"By the way, Jonesy, I spoke to the Polish army people in charge of the vehicles. The only truck I could talk them out of is an ambulance, but the more I think about, it could be just the thing. We can gut it, have room for our equipment, and be able to keep some of the sand out of it. We can put a rack on the top of it and carry more there with a tarp to cover it up. We need to make racks inside to keep smaller stuff. I want to be able to stay inside it, if possible, in the sand storms."

"I don't know, Reggie. I thought we wanted the half-track truck to get across the sand."

"Oh sorry," Reggie says, "the ambulance has the same tracks as the trucks. The only difference is instead of an open bed, it's enclosed, a big box on the back, and I think more to our purpose. I'm going to Poland to pick it up."

"Do you want some company?"

"Sure," Reggie says, "I'm glad you asked. We'll be going to Warsaw in Poland to pick up the truck, and then we'll drive it up to the port of Gdynia to ship it home. It's supposed to be brand new. The army wants more of the transport trucks. The officer I talked to said they would be happy to sell the ambulance so he could order another transporter. I'll arrange the trip and we should be able to leave on the next ship."

Early the next morning the two Special Branch men are back. They want to take Reggie to London. Reggie comes downstairs in a robe to see them.

"I am not going with you to London; I have arrangements to make in order to pick up the vehicle I need to make your trip."

"I'm sorry, sir, but I have orders to bring you in. S is angry that you did not report as he asked."

"You can call your Mr. S and tell him I'm not coming. He neglected to give me a way to contact him.

I can give him reports but I can tell you this; they will not be on a daily basis, that's just not possible. I'm going to be gone for ten or twelve days to get the truck. Come on, you can use the phone in the library and I'll get you some coffee while you call."

When Reggie returns with coffee, the man phoning S motions him to take the receiver.

Reggie takes the phone and says hello into the receiver.

He rolls his eyes and holds the phone away from his ear for a moment.

"You needn't shout, I can hear you from across the room. You didn't give me a number to contact you before I left."

As Reggie listens to S, he looks at the two Special Branch men and grimaces. His hand tightens around the receiver and his face darkens. The two Special Branch men blanch as Reggie shouts into the phone.

"That will be quite enough. If you cannot speak without yelling, I'm going to hang up. I've spoken to my attorneys and you will be receiving a visit from an officer of the American Embassy. You seem to have forgotten that both my mother and I have dual citizenships."

Without waiting for a reply, Reggie returns the receiver to its cradle.

Reggie turns to the Special Branch men, "I'll write a report for S to go back with you. Make yourselves comfortable. I'll be a few minutes."

After typing a brief report detailing his plans to pick up the truck, Reggie seals it in an envelope, and hands it to one of the man. He walks with them to the front door.

"Next time you fellows make the trip here, if you call first, I'll have breakfast for you."

One of the men starts down the stairs to the car; the other man turns to Reggie and says, "You've put a bee in S's bonnet sir. I hope you know what you're doing."

"As they say in America, we'll be jake. Have a good trip back gentlemen."

Later in the day, Reggie immerses himself in the necessary arrangements for him and Clive Parry-Jones to make their trip to and from Poland. Building a new vehicle and detailing all of the plans in anticipation for a new adventure are just the things that Reggie likes to keep life exciting.

Chapter 4

The ship leaves Dover in heavy seas. The four-day long trip is a tough one for both Reggie and Clive. Both men eat little and spend much of the trip tossed about in their bunks. After what seems to be much longer than four days, the ship slows its incessant rolling and makes way into Gdynia harbor. In contrast to most ports, Gdynia is very modern; it has recently undergone a massive build to export Poland's coal.

Reggie and Clive are eager to get off the ship and take the train to Warsaw. The almost 200-mile trip will give them a chance to eat and stretch their legs. Clive's unsteady walk to the train is a source of good fun for Reggie to jibe him.

"Haven't got your land legs yet, Jonesy? You have that peculiar gait of a duck out of water."

"Yes, hah, hah," Clive complains, "you have a very queer color of green about you too, Bobo old man."

"Uh oh," Reggie replies, "I see I've hit a sore spot, sorry old sport. Come on let's wobble down to the dining car. I'm beginning to feel like I could eat a horse."

Arriving in Warsaw the travel-weary men leave the train to take a cab to their hotel. After checking in and washing up, Reggie suggests they have an early dinner and turn in for a good night's sleep. They walk into the dining room of the old hotel and Reggie welcomes the sights and pungent smells of a wonderful three star restaurant. Clive slaps his hand over his heart in a exaggerated manner and exclaims, "I say old man, what is that smell?"

Reggie laughs. "It's called Bigos, a stew with sauerkraut, and pork; the taste is milder than it smells. I think it's one of the things that kept my father coming back here. Try some Zrazy, you'll love it, bacon and mushrooms wrapped in sirloin beef. Enjoy good food while you can old sport, the desert will not be so kind."

Over their first whisky in days, Reggie outlines the next day's plan.

"The vehicle yard is on the other side of town, but I wanted to stay here because my father always liked this place. I came here a lot on his business trips. Anyway, we'll take a cab to the compound and check out the truck. I have no doubt it will be as the commandant said, he was an old friend of father's. I have the bank draft to give them, and we can be on our way back to Gdynia by noon. With our new truck fitted out as an ambulance, it means we have the six-cylinder engine. We should be able to get maybe forty miles an hour out of it. With any luck, we can be in Gdynia tonight and load it aboard ship tomorrow."

"Sounds good to me, Reggie. Let's have a nightcap and turn in."

The morning finds the two men rested and ready to get out in the cool morning sunlight. After a quick breakfast, they take a taxi over the Vistula River. A thick mist rises from the river's banks. Shafts of sunlight penetrate the mist to reflect off the water's surface.

The commandant, a tall man resplendent in his gold-braided uniform with a perfect waxed mustache, meets Reggie and Clive at the compound. After reminiscing over coffee with Reggie, he takes them to the ambulance. The vehicle is brand new; the only mileage is from the drive to Poland from the factory. Reggie presents the commandant with the bank draft and politely declines an invitation to stay for dinner. Reggie shakes the commandant's hand and says, "I am sorry sir, but we have to be off to catch the ship back to England."

"I am sorry also, Reggie. I was looking forward to catching up on your latest adventures. Your father was always in a hurry to be off on his next challenge too. I still miss him. So are you after Mali gold in the Sahara or some other treasure?"

Reggie stops with driver's door open, and turns back to the commandant, "Mali gold sir? I did not think there was anything in the Sahara but endless sand."

"Come my boy, the sands of the desert cannot be the prize that beckons you. There have long been rumors of buried gold on the trade routes through the desert. I heard the legend of buried gold many years ago.

"A tribe of thieves attacked a caravan. The leader of the caravan spotted the thieves following them. He took some men and buried some 400 kilos of gold near an oasis. The thieves later fell on them and killed most of the men and made off with the camels and trade goods. Apparently, a few of the men lived to tell the tale. When you called about the truck I assumed you must be after the gold, or maybe you are after oil."

BOBO'S RAID

"I like the story sir," Reggie says. "Clive and I really are going because we didn't complete our last trip there. I read about the Citroëns and thought we could try them in the desert. We have plans to make our own vehicles for the British army."

The old commandant laughs. "Well no matter, I understand the apple falls close to the tree. Good luck to you my boy."

Reggie familiarizes himself with the truck's various controls and levers, and is soon on the way to the port of Gdynia. After three hours behind the wheel, they look for a place to stop for lunch.

After a trip to the restaurant's wash room and a quick lunch of soup and bread, Clive leaves the restaurant to start his first stint at driving the truck. Reggie waits at the counter to pay for the food. As Clive passes an alley, an arm reaches out and pulls him back into the alley. Clive loses his balance; falling backwards he bangs his head against the alley's iron corner protector. Two men pull Clive's inert body farther into the darkness of the alley.

Reggie comes out of the restaurant and goes to the truck. Pulling on the passenger door latch he finds the door locked. Reggie peers into the cab of the truck looking for Clive. He staggers backward as arms circle his chest and pull tight forcing the air from his lungs. While still in the fierce grip, a second man with a pistol steps in front of Reggie and demands the keys to the truck.

In a clipped cockney accent the bandit demands," I'll av' them keys."

"I don't have them. My friend is going to drive, he has the keys," Reggie gasps.

The man in front of Reggie tells the man holding Reggie to go find the keys on Clive.

"What have you done to my friend?" Reggie demands.

The gunman raises his pistol and says, "Don't do nothing stupid mate. Your friend just got some of what you're gonna get."

The other attacker returns and holds out the keys for the gunman to see.

"Righto," the gunman says, "'Old on to our highbrow friend here. We need to teach him a lesson before we take his truck."

While one man pulls Reggie's arms behind his back, the gunman puts the pistol away and fits a set of brass knuckles over his right hand.

With the man holding Reggie's arms, the Count cannot dodge the blow he sees coming. The brass knuckles scrape across his cheek as he pulls his head back away. A fist digs into his stomach and the brass knuckles slam down on his head. The arms holding Reggie's arms fall away and the Count crumples to his knees. Reggie fights to stay conscious; he puts his arm up to ward off the blows he knows are coming. He hears a loud crack and a scream. A hand tugs his arm helping him to stand up.

"Are you all right old man?" Clive asks, blood running down his cheek as he looks into the face of his friend. Reggie, still dazed, sees the man who hit him lying on the ground writhing in pain. He turns around to see the other bandit out cold on the sidewalk.

"What in the hell happened, Jonesy?"

"I don't know Reg, I guess these guys were going to rob us. One of these bums must have knocked me out, I felt someone rummaging through my pockets. When I got to my feet and out of the alley, I saw two of them with you. I found a piece of lumber in a pile back there and clubbed the guy that was holding you. When he dropped you, the man that was beating you tried to get a pistol out of his pocket. I swung the board as hard as I could and broke his arm before he could get the gun up. Let's call the police, you need to get your face looked at too."

"Jonesy my friend, you're a champ, but you look a mess. You may notice you have blood dripping from your chin. Let's get these guys out of sight; I want to find out who these monkeys are before we give them to the police. You grab the man with the broken arm and I'll drag the other into that alley."

In the seclusion of the alley Reggie asks the man with the broken arm who he works for.

"I ain't talk'n geeza."

Clive walks into the alley with the pistol the man dropped. He points it at the man's head. The bandit turns his head away and screams.

Reggie winks at Clive. "We don't want to kill him here if we can help it. I don't want to have to drag these bums back to the river to dump them. Why don't we just break his other arm for now and if that doesn't convince him to talk we can go to work on his friend."

Clive picks up the piece of lumber he used before and stands over the bandit.

"Grab his arm Reg, I'm gonna break it in two."

"No! I'll tell, I'll talk. Them Gavvers ain't gonna help me none. Some castle blokes come round with some dirty work for me and me mates sometimes. This bloke says you need a hard lesson. He says take your truck and give you a beatin'. He says we can sell the truck and keep the money."

"What's a "castle bloke"?" asks Reggie.

The bandits eyes are rolling back in his head, he is barely conscious. Clive kicks the mans foot and says, "Answer the man, what's a castle bloke? Who sent you after us?"

The man shakes his head. "I don't know. They got some fancy badges, Special Branch or the like. They come 'round in a big Humber car."

Reggie wipes his face and looks at the blood on his handkerchief, "Okay Jonesy, I'll go call the police, you watch these bums. When I get back, you need to go back in the restaurant and get that cut on your head cleaned up. If you feel up to it, I want to get back to England and talk to our special "castle" friends. I think Mr. S is the man that needs a hard lesson. I want this gentleman to give the Polish police an official statement that I can take back to England with us."

Chapter 5

Clive and Reggie return to England and spend a few idyllic days with their wives and friends playing with the new half-track ambulance. They go on picnics after traveling over rough fields and fording creeks. The steep rocky banks of the creeks hold little challenge for the truck. Reggie takes great delight in showing off his new toy.

The end of the week brings a cold front and rain; with the damp cold come the two Special Branch men. Reggie meets the men in the foyer with his mackintosh on ready to go with them to London.

S keeps Reggie waiting in the now-familiar little room. Reggie has the feeling someone is watching him. He puts his feet up on another chair and contents himself with a small book he takes from his pocket. The door to the room opens before he reads the first page. A Special Branch man is at the door to bring him to S.

S sits behind his desk. He looks up to tell the man that escorted Reggie in to leave them. S shuffles the paperwork on his desk and without looking at Reggie says, "Give me your report, Bobrowski."

Reggie lays the Polish police report on the desk and sits down in a chair.

S looks up from the papers, "What's this? I did not tell you to be seated."

"It's a report," Reggie replies, "And I didn't ask to be seated. You might want read the report, I'm rather anxious to get your reaction."

S picks up the report and quickly reads it. "So you foiled a robbery, do you think that entitles you to something?"

"Ah my dear Mr. S, I thought that would be your reaction. You did not have anything to do with it, is that it?"

"Of course I did Count, or is it Bobo? Sounds a clown's name to me. I am the director here. You offer no challenge to me. You need a lesson in respect for authority, my authority. I will rule you, boy. You may have been lucky to escape those pub scum lads, but you will come to heel now."

"I think you've read too much of Dickens, S. Apparently, you learned nothing from him. I sent copies of that report to my attorney and the American Embassy."

S selects a cigar from the box on his desk and goes through an elaborate ritual to light it. He leans back in his chair and blows a long stream of smoke into the air.

"You still do not understand who you are dealing with, do you? I got where I am today by always taking decisive action. Most people fear me. The men who matter in this government know I rule with a steel hand and appreciate that fact.

"I think you need some hard time to teach you manners. I'm going to send you to one of our training camps in Scotland. We have a place for misfits on one of the Orkney Islands. I should think 30 days will put you right."

BOBO'S RAID

"Before you swell up and try sending me off, I have another letter for you."

"Believe me, Bobo, you have nothing that would interest me. Keep your letter; you may need it to keep you warm in Scotland if you can keep it dry."

Reggie takes the letter from his pocket and lays it on S's desk. The coat of arms of his majesty's government is prominent at the top of the paper.

S flicks ash from the tip of his cigar, he blows on the lighted end and studies the glow with satisfaction. He looks to Reggie's face with a smirk of triumph. Reggie tips up the letter to show the coat of arms.

The smirk fades; S snatches the letter from Reggie. "What the deuce is this?" As S reads the letter his jaws crush the cigar, the broken end dips toward his chest. A moment later, he stands from his chair and throws the letter to the desk. "This is outrageous. How do you come by a letter from the Prime Minister?"

Reggie picks up the letter and returns it to his coat pocket. "Did I forget to mention that Mr. MacDonald and my father were friends? The PM is well aware of your questionable methods. I must say he is not very complimentary in your regard. As he states in the letter I will be responsible only to his office from this date. I plan to go to Algeria and watch the Germans, but my reports will be to Mr. MacDonald's office."

"Get out of my office, Bobrowski, before I have you in irons. You have not heard the last of this, you little popinjay. We'll see who wins here, get out!"

Reggie walks toward the door; he turns before he goes out and says to S, "I don't see much respect for you from anyone I talk to. Respect must be earned not just demanded."

"Get out! Get out! Get out! You insolent clown," S screams. He yanks the ruined cigar from his mouth and hurls it at Reggie, who quickly closes the door. The cigar explodes into showers of sparks when it hits the door; burning embers scatter across the room.

Chapter 6

Reggie and Clive, dressed in coveralls, are working on the Citroën at the Reading country house. The old carriage house has undergone a complete remodeling in order to become an automotive workshop. The men poured a smooth level concrete floor and outfitted the spacious shop with a huge hydraulic lift. Clive and Reggie did most of the work themselves. The men were like two boys in a toy store buying the tools and metal working machines for the shop.

The men modified the engine and drive train of the half-tracked vehicle for more speed. They extended the box forming the ambulance section and added shelves for their supplies, then made a framework atop the box to carry more equipment and extra fuel. The equipment stored on top will be the lightest in weight. A rope laced through grommets secures a canvas tarp to the framework. The canvas will cover the equipment and help insulate the interior from the terrific heat of the desert. The men are delighted with the work and the planning of their new adventure.

In the afternoon, Ally and Fay set up a table and chairs for lunch in the carriage house. The two wives repeatedly announce lunch is ready, their words falling on deaf ears. The men are lying under the truck absorbed in conferring on a drive train component.

Ally tugs on the Count's pant legs, "Come on, Reggie we're hungry. Lunch is ready; you and Clive have plenty of time to play with your truck."

Reggie, startled by the tug on his pants, bangs his head on the bottom of the truck. He slides out rubbing his head. Fay and Ally look at each other and laugh. Reggie has black grease where he banged his head that he is rubbing and spreading over his forehead.

"I see now why people call them grease monkeys," Ally says.

Clive comes around the truck, and when he sees Reggie, he, too, joins in the laughter.

Reggie still rubbing his head says, "What in the deuce is so funny?"

Ally takes Reggie's hand and leads him to the washroom.

After lunch the men are back to work on the truck. As the wives gather the plates and leftovers, a motorcycle powers up the long gravel driveway. A messenger dismounts in front of the carriage house and walks to the open doors.

"I have a message from Downing street for Count Bobrowski."

Reggie, hearing the motorcycle, walks from the garage to the messenger, rubbing his hands clean on a cloth.

"I'm Bobrowski, lad, are you going to wait for a reply?"

"Yes sir, if you would be so kind."

"Ally, would you please fix the lad some tea? I'll just be a moment." Reggie takes the message into the house and reads that the PM wants to meet with him in

BOBO'S RAID

London. The Count writes his reply on the Bobrowski letterhead and returns it to the messenger.

Morning brings frost to the countryside. The Count gets up early and after toast and coffee with Ally, he is ready to drive into London. Ally stands on her tiptoes to wrap a cotton muffler around Reggie's neck and to give him a kiss.

"Bobo, are you really going to wear that awful hat to see the Prime Minister?"

"What do you mean awful? It is colorful and the ear flaps will keep my ears warm."

Ally shakes her head. "The colors are dreadful, my dear. I think you must be color blind. You are going to see the Prime Minister; you should have some dignity. You could take the train into London and wear a good suit and hat."

"The PM has known me since I was a child, Ally. Besides Clive and I have just finished some work on the Riley. I want to give it a rip on the way. The morning is sparkling with frost and the drive in will be invigorating."

Reggie slides down in the seat of his Brooklands Riley. The little car is a brightly polished light-blue color. The chrome radiator grill and headlights gleam. The white wire wheels and black tires are nearly as tall as the low rakish bodywork. There are no doors or top on this car. When seated behind the steering wheel Reggie can touch the ground with his hand. The Count loves the feel of the nimble little car on the narrow country roads. After warming up the engine, Reggie motors down the driveway. Ally can hear the engine's exhaust note rise when Reggie reaches the main road.

The morning wind is cold and bites at Reggie's face. He and Clive have modified the engine's compression to run a methanol fuel. More compression equals more power. The smell of the burned fuel and the aroma of castor oil the engine uses as lubricant are heady scents that always bring to Reggie's mind the early mornings at the racetrack. The fresh start to a day when the racing engines first fire up and the morning's air fills with the promise of excitement.

Reggie knows the road well, and on some deserted stretches, he opens the throttle to feel the car respond with a burst of speed. He is pleased with the car's performance and the easy drive into the outskirts of London. After climbing from the Riley, Reggie looks back on the car with pride and goes contentedly on to his appointment.

The Prime Minister does not keep Reggie waiting long and graciously greets him. They exchange small talk before going into the office. Reggie is surprised to see Sir Benton Smyth sitting in a chair by the PM's desk. Smyth turns in his chair to grin at the Count's surprise. Reggie decides to make the best of it and goes to Smyth's chair to shake hands. Smyth does not stand or offer his hand.

This does not escape the PM's notice, and he says, "My dear Sir Smyth, I do hope you have not forgotten your manners."

Smyth reluctantly stands and grabs Reggie's hand in a bone-crushing grip. Reggie returns the grip and the men stand staring at each until both are aware of how awkward the clasp is. The PM watches with some bemusement.

BOBO'S RAID

"Gentlemen I have a busy schedule today, I suggest we get down to business. Please be seated. Reggie I asked you here to finalize plans for your… let's say expedition. Sir Smyth asked to be here, he would like to make a point or two. He wants a representative from his office to accompany you. I feel he has a good point. He tells me you have steadfastly refused to cooperate with him, and I want to clear the air. This is serious business; I do not expect this to turn into a jaunt for your pleasure, Count."

Reggie's knuckles turn white gripping the arms of the chair. He stands up and blurts out, "Enough." He looks at Smyth who is almost rubbing his hands enjoying Reggie's anger.

Reggie embarrassed by his own outburst sits down and apologizes to the PM. "Excuse me sir, I do not mean to disrespect your office. Mr. S's method of direction is tyrannical. He expects total obedience without question; he tried to deny me the tools I will need to be successful. The order I refused was to take my wife to Algeria with me. I will not take my wife into the desert and put her in harm's way. I have to add that S has done nothing so far to be helpful. Indeed, he has gone out of his way to sabotage the mission. The example is Poland, as I explained to you earlier.

"I have purchased, with my own money, the truck and the equipment I think we need to follow the Jerrys. Our truck is the best in the desert and we can outmaneuver them if we need to.

"The only thing the man has ever said to me that made sense was that I owe England a debt for giving me a home. I promise you, sir, that I will do my best to give you all the information you need. I am taking this expedition on with all seriousness.

"To that end, I am studying the geology oil men use to find oil deposits. I have friends in America that have looked at the potential oil fields in Algeria, and sent me their maps. I know there was an oil discovery in the Chelif Basin in 1892 in the northwest of Algeria. The Americans think the main oil fields could be in the eastern desert portion of Algeria. They say that the country could have vast stores of petrochemicals, but that the problems and costs of getting any product out of the country are prohibitive.

"Germany may have a different plan for Algerian oil. We know they are reliant on foreign oil for their industry, so they need any oil they can find. Maybe they are not concerned with the costs of getting oil out of the country. As you can see, Mr. Prime Minister, I have taken this trip seriously, and I will continue to do my best to bring you the results you need.

"What I need from S are the radios he promised and where I can find the German exploration team. If he needs to send a man with us, so be it. I will be in command and his man will have to understand that."

Reggie looks directly at Sir Smyth and says to the PM, "If you can keep him from interfering, I will report any oil the Germans find."

S can take no more; he stands up to tower over Reggie. "Who the hell do you think you are? You're Bobo the clown, boy. Do you think for one moment that I am going to stand for any more of your insolence? This is my operation… I am in command. I don't give a damn who you know. You will take your orders from me and like it."

BOBO'S RAID

The Prime Minister, still seated behind his desk, watches the two men spar. Without rising from his chair his voice booms out in a cold steel tone, "Sit down Benton. I will oversee this operation. Reginald will report to me and I will pass on any pertinent information to your office, Smyth. In this circumstance I will be the buffer between you two. We need to know what Jerry is up to; Hitler is becoming more and more powerful and threatening. We need to keep our eyes on the Germans. Your egos are not important here. If they find oil, their war machine could be unstoppable.

"When can you be ready to go Reggie?"

"As soon as I have the radios, and the information on the Germans' location, sir."

"Very good, Reggie. Benton, get Count Bobrowski whatever he needs. I do not expect any further trouble between you and Reggie. Do we understand each other?"

Benton Smyth, sitting forward in his chair with his fists clenched, looks at each man. A vein in his forehead throbs. "Look MacDonald, this is not your territory. I know what is best. This is my job. Your ah… friend here is not right for this operation. I can put together a team from my group and take command. The Count can turn over the equipment he has and I can get underway."

MacDonald shows signs of agitation. "There will be no more discussion, Benton. I find your disrespect of my office deplorable. It is I who am in command! You will do well to keep that in your head."

In calmer voice the PM turns to Reggie. "You have your orders. Reggie. I will see that you have what you need and any support you need while you are in the field. That is all gentlemen. You are excused."

Reggie stands and shakes the PM's hand. Benton Smyth waits until Reggie is at the door and says to the PM, "This is a mistake MacDonald." He turns away and follows Reggie out.

Mr. S closes the door and hastens to catch Reggie in the hall. He swings his swagger stick hard and slaps the back of Reggie's legs. Reggie stumbles forward and then spins around to S, his face contorted with rage. He grabs Smyth's swagger stick raising it over his head to strike. Mr. S cowers back raising his arms over his face.

Chapter 7

Two of the guards stationed in the hall move quickly to separate Reggie and Smyth.

Smyth screams at the guard to take his hands off him. "Get that mad man away from me. Did you see him try to attack me?"

Prime Minister MacDonald opens the door to his office to see what the commotion in the hall is.

Smyth struggles out of the guard's grip. "Your idiot friend attacked me, he's crazy. I want him in irons... now!"

MacDonald sees Reggie twisting the swagger stick in his hands. "What on earth has gotten in to you Reggie?"

"Er, excuse me sir," the senior hall guard asks MacDonald, "May I have a word sir?"

"Yes, Niles, if you think it important at this moment."

The guard closes the door to the PM's office behind them.

A short time later, the PM opens the office door. "Count, I apologize for my mistake. Please give the stick back to Sir Smyth and be on your way. We will talk very soon. Thank you for coming."

Reggie breaks the stick over his knee and drops the pieces to the floor. The PM shrugs, then motions for the guards to bring Smyth into his office. S struggles between the two men. "Take your bloody hands off me."

Reggie walks to his car, looking forward to the drive back to Reading. Sitting in the little Riley, he finds that the seat presses against the back of his legs where S struck him. Working the brake and clutch pedals in London traffic feels as if a coarse rope is sawing at the back of his legs. Out of traffic, the road opens to let the Riley find some speed. Reggie enjoys the improved performance of the car and sails home leaving thoughts of the man called S behind.

Chapter 8

Back in Reading, Reggie and Clive are putting the final additions on the Citroën truck. The garage, warmed by a coal stove, is cutting the cold of the English winter. The men finish the cabinets inside the box cabin, securing special doors on the cabinets to keep items inside while the truck jostles over rough terrain. Some of the shelves have fishing net strung to hold equipment. Two simple framed bunks fold back to the sides of the box. The men fitted a table at the front of the box with rubber isolators to mount the radios and protect them from vibration.

Reggie phones the Prime Minister several times to find out when he can get the radios. The PM tells Reggie that he funded Smyth's department for the radios and was waiting for S to deliver them to his office.

Reggie, frustrated with the delay, makes another call to MacDonald.

"Sir I have ordered radios for my Reading home and an aircraft set for the Citroën. I want to be in place in Algeria while we are still in the winter months.

"We can do our set up work on a base of operation and spread the word that we are there to test the truck. Perhaps we can start the rumor mill working about roaming the desert looking for lost gold. I think that could give us a good cover story. We can play being there for a lark and throw off any suspicion that we are following the Germans.

"I need information on the German exploration. I do not think it would be wise to ask after them when we get to Algeria. I would like to know where they have a base, and any information you have on the men in the group. Clive and I will be ready to leave in a week's time, sir."

"I'm sorry for the delay Reggie. Smyth is dragging his feet on this. I understand you need to get going. We should have been in place before this. The Germans may have already found oil deposits we will not know about. I do have other intelligence sources that will put together a dossier on everything we know about the Germans. You will have it in two days. We will monitor your radio transmissions from here. We should have some code phrases in case you need help. Let's meet before you go and we'll firm up any loose ends."

The following week is busy with the installation of the new Belmont small aircraft-type radio receiver and transmitter sets in the truck. Both men practice using the truck's radio; the wives delight in learning to use their bigger, more powerful sets installed in the house. Reggie purchased a massive radio that can receive worldwide signals and set up a dedicated room in the library. Both couples learn the magic of the airwaves; tuning, signing on and off, and radio speak. There is much to learn in a short time.

Soon Reggie goes to London to meet with the PM and make the final preparations.

The PM hands Reggie a file. "This is the dossier on the German oil exploration men you wanted. I have spoken to Sir Smyth several times. I am quite disappointed with his behavior; however he has an operative in place in Touggourt with a radio set. I'm afraid that is all the cooperation we will see from him."

Reggie, seated before the PM's desk, takes a sip of his tea. "I think we will be better served by his lack of help sir. I will do my best to get the information you want. If you will pardon a suggestion sir, I would like to see a man from your office in Touggourt. I will send some innocent sounding information to Reading on the radio that you can monitor. However if you need to issue special instructions it would arouse suspicion on our radio. I don't trust Smyth sir; I would like to make sure of our communications."

"Reggie I can not send a man to work against another British department. I can put a man in Touggourt, but he will have to work with Smyth's man."

"I understand sir; I feel better knowing one of your men is on my side. Thank you for your help. Clive and I will be on the next boat to Philippeville. We will unload the Citroën and head straight to Touggourt. If your man can fly in, he will be in place well before we get there."

The PM rises from behind his desk and shakes Reggie's hand. "Take care Count. I appreciate your help in this. I will have a man in place you can trust. Believe me this is important work, Reggie. If we know where the Germans have oil reserves, we can block their use in wartime. I am sure from Hitler's posturing that war is inevitable.

"I have no doubt that the Nazis on this mission could be ruthless if they think you are following them. Read the dossier and know your enemy. This mission could indeed put you in harm's way."

Back in Reading, Reggie and Clive run the Citroën through some final testing with the truck now fully loaded. They make some changes to where some items are stored to balance the weight distribution. Satisfied that they are ready to tackle the Sahara, Reggie books passage to Philippeville, Algeria.

Reggie and Clive watch from the ship's upper deck as a large crane lifts the Citroën, supported by a wooden pallet, from the dock. The truck swings precariously in the wind as the crane's crew struggles with guide ropes to lower it into the hold. The weight of the truck pulls the men across the deck; two men fall and let go of the ropes. Wood splinters as the pallet under the truck crashes against the ship's railing. The crane operator drops the truck heavily to the deck before it swings back out over the dock.

Reggie and Clive run down to the deck, both wondering if the trip is over before it starts.

Chapter 9

Rushing across the deck, they see that the heavy wooden pallet broke up on one end when it hit the deck. A beam with a jagged end has thrust up into the left side track. The crew chief surveying the damage apologizes to Reggie. He directs the deck crew to get to work repairing the pallet, and storms away to find out what the crane operator has to say.

Reggie stands aside as a crewman saws through the heavy beam and pulls it away. He squats down to look at the track and running gear. "I don't see any damage other than the track. This thing is certainly one tough piece of kit."

Clive runs his hand over the wrinkled fender above the track. "Any doubt I had about this bit doing the job just vanished. She's done us proud, Reg."

Reggie asks the deck chief if they can replace the track while the truck is in the hold.

"Sorry sir, after we close the hatches no one is allowed in the holds. They will not be uncovered until we reach port."

Reggie turns to Clive and says, "I don't like the idea of sitting on a wharf in Philippeville fitting a new track. I'm anxious to get on our way before we run into any interference from our Mr. S. He'll know when the ship comes into port. I'd feel better if we could just get going once the truck gets on the ground. Anyway, I'll get another track sent out. I don't want to use up our spares before we even get to Touggourt. Let's get our gear up to the cabin; we'll get squared away and find the saloon."

The motor freighter, *Kay Manor*, is a 5000-ton cargo ship with a fifty-passenger capacity. The smart styling of the ship's hull is based on the classic ocean liners of the day. Built by a Danish shipyard, powered by a 7000-horsepower B&W diesel through twin screws, she has a fast cruising speed of 15 knots. The ship's normal trade route is through the Mediterranean to the Black Sea and returning to England with Asian goods and passengers. In these days of world-wide depression, the trade route is slowed to the point that any profit gained from trade is welcome. Coal once regarded as dirty cargo for this ship is now an essential commodity to trade.

Reggie and Clive find their cabin to be neat and clean. They have two high-sided beds and a private bathroom in the surprisingly large rooms. Buoyed by the simple elegance of the cabin, the men decide to repair to the bar.

The bar and the dining room are in the same space under the ship's bridge. There are twelve good sized tables with four to six club chairs per table. The bar is situated by the aft wall. Forward, a row of large square windows add light and expanse to the room, giving the diners a view of the vast sea over the ship's bow.

Reggie walks to the windows to look out over the two forward holds. He watches men on deck finish loading cargo and lock down the hatches.

BOBO'S RAID

The land lines are cast off and the ship's big diesels send a slight vibration through the ship as the propellers are engaged and bite into the murky water of the port.

Clive calls out to Reggie from his seat at the bar. "Gin and tonic's at the ready old sport."

Reggie turns back to the bar. He takes a seat next to Clive and sips the cool drink, the tonic water still fizzy.

Several men come in and sit around tables; the bar men are busy ferrying drinks to thirsty travelers. Conversations in several languages spark life into the space.

"You can relax, old man, we're on the way. No sign of your friend Mr. S."

"Jonesy, I am happy to be on our way, but I doubt we'd know if S had a man on board to watch us."

"That's a lovely thought. I did bring my Webley. It's in my suitcase. Did you pack that Colt cannon you favor?"

"My cannon, as you say, Browning's finest, is a very reliable weapon my friend. The heft of it in your hand gives you a sense of security. And yes, it is in the cabin. I don't expect any trouble from S that would require the use of weapons, but it can't hurt to be prepared."

Clive rises his glass. "I'll drink to that."

"Seems you have," Reggie signals to the bartender. "Your glass is empty, this one's on me."

The bartender pulls the towel from his shoulder and polishes the bar in front of the two men. "What'll you have, gents?"

"Another gin and tonic for my friend here, I'm still working on mine. I'm Reggie, this is my friend Clive. I must say I didn't expect the ship to be so busy with passengers."

The bartender offers his hand. "Glad to meet you. My name's Roberts. I can tell you we're as busy as I've ever seen. I reckon the state of the economy has pushed more people our way. We don't travel the usual liner routes, but our fares are much less expensive. The ship's owners and our captain run a real ship-shape vessel. A lot of our passengers are with us on almost every voyage. Where are you gents headed?"

Clive launches in on a full-color story of roaming the desert sands to perfect their truck before he stammers to a halt under Reggie's withering stare.

Roberts grins at the men. "Desert roamers are you? I hope you didn't buy a Mali gold treasure map."

Reggie replies in mock surprise. "Mali gold? Can't say we've heard of it. No, the truck's the ticket. We have some innovations we're sure will make desert travel much better. The coming years will bring more exploration for minerals, oil, and trade goods. The places on this earth that are unexplored are shrinking. The deserts are huge expanses that cry out for exploration."

"You sold me, mate." Roberts slaps the towel over his shoulder before he moves to serve another thirsty soul.

"Sorry Reggie, I let my mouth get ahead of me again."

"No, it's all right, might be just perfect in fact. Roberts probably knows everything there is to know on this ship. Let him think we're just a couple of country bumpkins looking for fool's gold. We can chat him up later to see if he knows about anyone looking for oil in the desert.

"We don't want to sell the gold story too hard. We could get ourselves in trouble if some bandits think we're on to something. We don't want to be followed about while we're trying to follow the Jerrys."

The sun goes low in the western sky as the ship begins the journey to make way south through the English Channel.

"How about something to eat? I'm going to turn in early and get some sleep while the sea's still calm."

Reggie and Clive take a table near one of the windows. Passengers in small groups begin to fill the tables. The level of noise rises as more hungry people file in. A confusing din of various languages adds a sense of chaos to the place. A thin, wire-haired man with a dimpled glass of beer approaches the table.

"Do you gentlemen mind if I join you? I understand you're English."

Clive and Reggie stand to greet the man.

"Please have a seat. This is Clive and I am Reggie."

"Pleased to meet you, I'm Gilbert Lewis. Call me Gil, everyone does. I saw you loading the Citroën; talk is you're going on a desert exploration in Algeria."

Reggie and Clive exchange a look of annoyance.

Gil smiles uneasily at the look and says, "Sorry fellows, word gets around fast on this ship. Everyone knows, or thinks they know, all the passengers' business."

"Well Gil," Reggie replies. "Let me set the record straight. We're taking the Citroën through the Sahara to test some new improvements we've made. We are also going to try to ascertain the feasibility of a railroad to exploit trade goods to the coastal ports. That's the plan, so maybe you can set the record straight."

Gil takes his hands from the beer mug, palms out. "Please don't take offense. Gossip is the main topic on this ship to while away the hours, there's not much else to do."

"That's okay Gil, I can see this ship would be a beehive of gossip with the diversity of passengers aboard. What kind of business are you in?"

Feeling somewhat relieved, Gil sits back in his chair takes a sip from his beer. "I'm a mechanical engineer; I work for a company in London that builds blast furnaces. We're helping the Turks build a steel mill. I take this ship to Turkey, work there for two weeks, and usually return back home on this ship for two weeks.

"But let me tell you, I do understand your annoyance. I've traveled back and forth on this ship for a year now, and the gossip is that I bring back more than just the hand woven rugs I sell when I get back home. That little treat has branded me as a smuggler to the point that customs has a good look at the rugs I bring back every trip. The money I make on the rugs is too good to pass up though."

Clive seems uninterested in the conversation and has his nose buried in the dinner menu, so Reggie responds.

"Sorry to hear that Gil, but that's just my point. We have a job to do and I don't want to have to fend off the locals or the authorities. I have to replace the track that was damaged on the Citroën when we get to Philippeville, and I don't want to waste time on customs and then have to do the repairs on the dock. The deck chief says no one is allowed in the holds after they lock them down. He won't let us do the work."

Gil grins and nods his head knowingly, "Getting into the hold your truck's stored in is not a big problem. If there is some wine or liquor stowed in the hold, a sailor will find it. I know a couple of boys that can get practically anything out of the hold as long as it won't be missed. Probably cost you less than a quid for one of 'em to get you in and out without anyone being the wiser."

Chapter 10

Regaled with Gil's hilarious tales of high adventure in Turkey, the men keep the bar open until early morning. Reggie and Clive get up late the next day, a bit worse for wear.

Bending over the sink, groaning at his reflection in the mirror, Clive tries to steady his hand as he puts razor to cheek. "When you were talking trains last night, did one run me over?"

Reggie, fumbling with shirt buttons, replies, "We should have stopped sooner; I was having so much fun listening to Gil's tales I completely forgot the time. Keeping the drinks coming seemed like good idea at the time."

Clive wipes the shaving cream from his face. "Where on earth does that man get all those stories? My head hurts when I think of how hard we laughed."

Reggie nods gently, "I can see why the ship's crew finds him so popular. I get the idea he's as entertaining to himself as he is to us. Let's go take a turn on deck, we'll get some lunch and be right as rain."

Clive, still at the mirror, but now tending to his razor wounds, says, "I hope that works."

After wolfing bacon and tomato sandwiches, washed down with numerous cups of coffee, the boys are stirring to life. They take some brisk laps around the deck and return to the dining room to have a cold beer.

BOBO'S RAID

Gilbert slumps in a short time later. He brings a tall glass of a reddish mixture from the bar to the table, and plops down in a chair, his hands cradling his head. Without looking up, he says in a weary voice, "Thank my dear lord and saviour for a calm sea. Why in the devil did you two make me drink like that?"

Reggie laughs, "I thought we did most of the drinking, you were too busy spinning yarns to do half the damage we did."

Gil takes a tentative sip of his drink, makes a sour face, and says, "You boys still want to go down in the hold to fix your truck? If I live long enough today, I think I can arrange it."

Clive looks at Reggie and says, "Not today Reg. I'll go tomorrow, but I'm not on for today."

Reggie brushes the beer's foam from his lip. "Can you put it on for tomorrow Gil?"

"I'll see what I can do; you'll not want to be down there in a rough sea. It's calm today, no tellin' about tomorrow."

"We'll take our chances; it'll be an early night for us. If you can make it for morning, we could be done by midday."

"If it's morning you want, it'll be before 4 o'clock. The mate'll have to be off duty and most of the ship's company still asleep."

Clive nods to Reggie. "That's okay with us. We'll leave you to your misery. Cheers mate."

Gil, his head cocked resting on one hand, replies. "Yeah thanks ... mates."

A steward delivers a note to the cabin from Gil. Reggie opens the envelope to read the note that simply states, "You're on."

Early the next morning Clive is waiting by the cabin door when he hears a soft tapping. He nods to Reggie, turns off the cabin's light and both men leave the cabin.

In the dim light they can make out a man who holds up a finger to the lips of his bushy face and motions them to follow. They follow the man down a companionway ladder onto the main deck and through a door into a long hallway. In the middle of the hallway they turn a sharp corner and descend farther into the ship's bowels.

As they descend, the steps become steeper so that they have to grasp the hand rails to keep their footing. The cones of light grow farther apart the deeper they go. Each man's shadow stretches and contracts as if they are chasing each other. To Reggie and Clive it seems a dizzying labyrinth of light-gray painted-steel companionways and steps that finally leads them to the end of one of the hallways. There is a small hatch bordered by a riveted plate that the furry-faced man works to unlatch. He opens the hatch and steps through.

Clive and Reggie see a light come on from inside the hatchway. The man's head appears and he motions them inside. The two men hunch over and step through the hatch to find a huge cavern of steel tiers. Each tier is piled high with crates and barrels of stored goods. Their heads swivel trying to capture the enormity of the space.

"Your truck's on the top level gents. It's dark in places so follow me."

These are the first words they have heard from the furry-faced man. They follow him as he leads them with his flashlight up several levels to their Citroën. At the truck, the man takes off his coat and seems to shrink several sizes. He is a small slender man with coal black hair covering his face and the back of his hands. Tufts of hair spring from the collar of his shirt.

"Me name's Colin; you can pay me now an' get on with your work. I've some shopping to do; I'll check back later to lead you out."

Reggie steps forward taking some change from his pocket. "Thanks Colin, we should just be a couple of hours. Will there be any problem with us leaving after daybreak?"

"Shouldn't be gov'ner. We'll separate at the 'atch and you can be on your merry way."

Colin takes a drawstring bag and the flashlight from his coat, and is off through the shadows to his shopping.

The lights in the hold, although bright, are arrayed far apart and cast dark shadows around the crates and the ship's massive steel structure.

"Let's get the lights set up, Clive. We'll do it just like we practiced back home. We can run them off the auxiliary batteries for now."

The men set to work getting the lights up, and take a spare track from the top of the truck.

Clive is setting up bottle jacks to lift the truck when all the ship's lights in the hold go off. The men have good light on their work but beyond their lights is nothing but a black hole.

For the first time since coming into the hold they really notice the motion of the ship and the eerie sounds of steel creaking and cargo shifting.

Clive stops and looks out of the light. "My God, it's just black. You think that little monkey Colin's a joker?"

"I don't know; he didn't seem the type. Don't go out of the light, there's no railing here, it's a long way down. I'll take a flashlight and see if I can find a light switch."

A small beam of light pierces the black from below them. Colin calls out from a lower tier. "Stay where you are gents, I'll go see why the lights are off."

"Let's get the track on, Jonesy. When Colin gets the lights back on, we can get out of here. I'm not so sure this was a good idea. I don't want to be down here with no light and have the sea go rough."

"Don't worry Reg, I won't let the booger man get you."

"Right, my champion, now I've nothing to fear as long as your booger man chases you, running for the exit."

"Ha, ha, hand me a torch, old man; I need to get under the truck to position the jacks."

Reggie opens the driver's side door and takes a flashlight from a pocket in the door.

"Here's a flashlight, old boy, I hope it'll do til' I get a torch fired up."

"Civilized men call them torches. Why would you cowboys from the wilds of America call them flashlights anyway? You have an answer for that?"

"They are called flashlights because the early ones had carbon element bulbs that would only work for a short time. So you had to switch them on and off all the time."

BOBO'S RAID

"I should have known you'd have an answer. Did you just make that up?"

"Why I thought you knew, us Yanks have all the answers. A torch is something you set on fire from the dark ages. I'll start getting the track off the front sprocket."

Colin comes into the circle of light cursing his light and whacking it against his palm. "Dammed torch keeps goin' out."

Clive nods at Reggie. "Civilized man."

Colin eyes both men with frown. "Someone's shut the bleedin' lights off from outside; I can't get 'em back on. The 'atches are dogged and locked from the outside too."

Both men ask at the same time. "So we're stuck down here?"

Colin puts down the bulging drawstring bag. "I've got to get back to me duty station. If the cap'in finds out I'm down here, it'll be me neck. I'll get out a vent duct and be back for you."

"You're sure to come back for us?" Clive asks.

"I've left me bag and coat; I'll 'ave to come back for 'em, won't I?"

The little man disappears out of the light, his flashlight searching back and forth across the black maw.

Clive says, "I hope that's not the last we see of him."

Reggie chuckles. "Don't worry old friend, I won't let the booger man get you."

Chapter 11

Clive wipes the sweat from his forehead; he and Reggie had just finished wrestling the new track in place. They sit on the edge of the pallet the truck rests on, staring out at the blackness.

"Wasn't like back at the garage Reg; getting it jacked up off this bloody pallet is a pain in the arse."

He glances at Reggie and turns back to study the blackness. "Why would someone lock the hatches from the outside? That little monkey man's been gone for a long time."

Reggie turns away from his own thoughts. "Steady on old man; I haven't the faintest why the hatches are locked. If Colin doesn't show up soon, we'll go have a look for ourselves. We have plenty of food and water, it's not like we'll starve. If we should have to stay here until we reach the first port, I'll have the captain's backside when we get out."

Clive pats his stomach and groans."I'm hungry, bloody hungry, and it's getting colder down here."

Reggie slaps his hands on his knees as he stands up. "Okay, we may be here awhile, let's make some coffee."

Clive gets to his feet. "I'll have tea thank you very much. Biscuits, I almost forgot we've got biscuits."

After their meal of tea and biscuits they are back to sitting on the pallet staring out into the black space.

BOBO'S RAID

"Well it's been hours now, I'm going to go find the hatch we came in and see if it's still locked. Maybe I can beat on it, make a lot of noise, and get someone to open it."

"I'll go with you."

"Stay here Clive; if Colin comes back while I'm gone, you need to be here. Have some more tea, I won't be gone long. If the hatch is still locked I'm not going to stay there very long. I'll come back and we'll beat on the hull with some wrenches till someone hears us."

Reggie's flashlight sends a small circle of light through the inky blackness in front of him as he searches for the ladder to the deck below them. The pure blackness is disorienting; after some wrong turns, he finds the next ladder and is on his way down when the ship's lights blaze on. Startled, Reggie's foot slips past the ladder's rung. He grabs at the ladder's railing but still bangs his shin hard against the missed steel rung. The flashlight falls from his hand and clatters to the steel deck below.

Looking down at the hole in his pant leg Reggie hears the dogs on the hatch unlatching and Colin's furry head pops through the opening.

Reggie, sitting on the ladder rubbing his shin yells, "What in the blue blazes took you so long?"

"Sorry gov'ner. By the time I got out the bleedin' vent'later, I 'ad to go on duty. I just snuck away to find the lights and come back for you. I couldn't rightly ask nobody where the switchbox for the lights was. 'Appens it's just by the 'atch. It's got a big S chalked on it."

Reggie inspecting his dented flashlight asks. "A big S, does that mean something to you? I mean is that the way a switchbox is usually marked?"

"No gov, means somebody jus' chalked it."

"Okay, let's go get my friend."

Back at the truck Reggie and Clive put away the camping equipment they brought out to cook water for their tea.

Colin puts on his coat and picks up the drawstring bag. "I'll be off now gov, I'm on duty, I reckon you can find your way out."

"Hold up, Colin." Reggie steps around the truck's pallet.

"Do you know who locked the hatches?"

"Can't say I do gov. Maybe some bloke playin' a joke."

"You have friends that would like you locked up down here?"

"Well some o' the boys know I can get out the vent'later. It's bleedin' 'ard job that. I'll have a ear offa me mates if'n it were one o' 'em."

"Let me know if you find out who locked us down here, I will want to talk with them. Here's a pound for your trouble Colin, thanks for coming back."

Colin beams, teeth white against a mass of black hair. He stuffs the money in his coat pocket. "Righto, I'll be findin' 'em. I'ad to come back for me stuff didn't I? Thanks gov."

Clive locks the doors to the truck and steps off the pallet. "I'm for a drink Reg. Let's be off, old man."

"I'll savor a drink with you old friend, after I've had a washup, and a change of clothes. Colin said someone chalked an S on the light box switch. I want to take a look at that on our way out."

Clive points his finger above his head. "You're thinking we've got friends in high places?"

"S means anything but friend to me. We need to try to find who it is before we get to port. We're going to want to check the truck again before we get to port. Make sure everything is locked and sealed."

With the ship's lights on, the trip to the ladder and the lower decks is quick and easy. Clive goes out first and Reggie switches the lights off inside the hold and goes out of the hatch.

As Reggie looks around the hatch, he says over his shoulder, "Colin said the switch was outside the hatch, you see anything?"

Clive does a slow turn looking over the walls. "Did you mean the box with a wooden handle on the side and a big S on it?"

Reggie looks to his right and sees a panel with a fire ax in it and next to it the switch box. "Oh, that light switch."

Clive shakes his head. "That might explain why we haven't won many races lately."

Reggie punches Clive on the shoulder. "Very funny, let's go."

After getting back to their cabin, washing up and changing clothes, the men are off to the dining room.

Out on deck the black sky is filled with a million stars; the men stop to take in the panorama. Clive puts his hands to his chest and takes a deep breath of sea air. "I'm happy to be out of that hold. We're lucky to still be in good weather."

Reggie smiles, walking with his head forward into the wind, hands in his pockets. "Too right, as you would say, Jonesy old boy. It could have been a bad time down there. Someone knew we were going down there. We need to be careful about what we talk about on this ship. I'm sure S has more in store for us.

"Look Jonesy, when we have dinner let's talk about staying in Philippeville after we dock. If S's man thinks we'll be there awhile maybe we can surprise him and get on our way before he can try something else."

They find the bar is elbow to elbow, raised voices and flushed faces of men and women all talking in different languages trying to be heard. Tobacco smoke spirals up to swirl around the ceiling fans. Clive and Reggie sit at a table in a corner away from the confusion.

Clive fidgets at the table trying to catch one of the waiters. "I'll go fight the crowd for a beer. If you can get a waiter order me the biggest steak they've got. You want a beer, something else?"

"A beer would be fine; the next time a waiter goes by I'll wrestle him to the ground."

Clive returns to the table with two beers. "Roberts had mercy on me and passed me these beers. He says with all the good weather people are at the bar first thing in the morning and some don't leave until he kicks them out at night."

Reggie takes a long pull on his beer. "I did tackle a waiter, but no steaks. He says the steaks are frozen and we have to place an order in the morning to get a steak for dinner. We're having lamb stew."

Gil Lewis appears at the table. "Mind if I join you?"

BOBO'S RAID

"Have a chair Gil; you'll have to fight for your own beer though."

To Reggie and Clive's surprise a waiter hustles over to the table to takes Gil's order.

"You gents ready for another beer?" he beams.

"You bet we're ready. How on earth do you manage that?" Reggie asks.

"I sometimes slip him a small rug on the return trips if he looks after me."

Clive says, "Can you get us a steak for dinner tonight?"

"Righto, how would you like it done mate?"

"Rare for me, Reggie likes his more done though."

Gil signals the waiter who hurries over to take the order.

"I heard you boys had a spot of bother."

Reggie finishes his beer. "News does travel fast on this ship. Who told you?"

"Blackie told me and gave me a message to pass along."

The men fall silent as the waiter sets down three beers on the table.

Reggie clicks his mug against the two others. "Thanks Gil. Who might Blackie be?"

"That's Colin, the mates call him Blackie. The way Colin tells it they tried calling him monkey boy at first. He says he thrashed every man that called him that, so Blackie is what stuck. Anyway he says he found a mate that saw a woman covered head to toe in an Arab get up following you blokes this morning. The mate followed for a while until the women surprised him at a turn in the companionway with a huge pistol she stuck in his face.

"Blackie says he's hearing scuttlebutt that someone paid the crane operator to drop your truck. He says the truck striking the railing was all that saved it from crashing down to the dock. Makes me wonder what kind of business you're really in."

Reggie replies quickly with a cover story. "I don't know why a woman would be interested in us. I did turn down a man who wanted us to take him in as a partner. The man stuck me crooked enough to screw into the ground. He was pretty unhappy with me when I turned him down. If we decide that there is a real market for a railway, I have investors I can trust."

Gil sits his beer mug on the table. "Well, one thing I've learned out here is to mind my own business. You'd do well to watch your backsides. That's all I can say."

"Thanks for the warning. Clive and I don't plan to ruffle any feathers. We were just talking about visiting the Roman ruins in Philippeville before we head south. Maybe we'll run into this Arab woman."

Chapter 12

The freighter stops at the ports of Oran, and then Algiers before the last Algerian port of Philippeville. Reggie confers with the ship's captain to make sure the truck is transferred to the dock undamaged. The captain personally oversees the successful transfer.

Gil Lewis walks with the men to the gangway to see them off.

"Have a good trip you two, it was nice to meet you. Where are going from here?"

Before Clive can answer, Reggie says, "We're going to hold up here a couple of days and see the sights. Maybe lie on the beach and soak up some sun before we set off. I don't expect we'll be seeing the sea again any time soon. It was nice to meet you Gil, thanks for taking care of us. Oh yeah, which way to the best beach?"

"Past the harbor, take the road east. Have a safe trip."

Reggie unlocks the truck on the dock and stows the bags while Clive opens the hood and checks the engine. Reggie gets in the cab to inspect the gauges. Clive gives him thumbs up and Reggie starts the engine. Reggie waves away the dock hands and drives the truck off the pallet. Clive gets in and they motor away from the dock.

Reggie turns the truck to the east and drives out of the docks into the brilliant sun rising high above the palm trees. As soon as the harbor fades in the distance Reggie turns the truck toward the south.

"I reckon about four days to Touggourt. We'll take it easy and stop in Biskra. When we get to Touggourt I want to see what S has in store for us. I hope the PM got a friend stationed for us so we don't have to rely on S's man.

We'll stop at the top of that range of hills and try out the radio. I can't wait for both of us to talk to the ladies. I think it's just as important to establish contact with Touggourt. We need some way to talk to our man without S's man getting in on it."

The men drive in three-hour shifts during the day and two-hour shifts at night. The road is good, some tarmac and some sections hard-packed ground. The night shifts are shorter due to the concentration it takes to stay on the unmarked sections of the road.

They find some changes from where they joined this same road on their last trip. The local governments have made improvements through small villages to make the road wider for automobile traffic. The trip, about 160 miles from Philippeville, goes from a warm sea to the snow-covered mountains and into Biskra.

Since France established Algeria as a colony, finding a good place to spend the night in Biskra at a European style hotel is not difficult. They have dinner in the hotel and turn in for the night.

Early the next morning they are on their way to Touggourt. After a brief vehicle check, Reggie settles into the driver's seat.

BOBO'S RAID

Clive climbs in and Reggie says with frost forming on his breath, "I called the CGT hotel in Touggourt, they'll be expecting us in the early hours of tomorrow. I've watched for anyone following us on the road. I didn't see anyone really interested in us. I think we got away without S's men following us."

Making the heater work better is one of their upgrades to ward off the cold; the men are snug in the Citroën after the truck warms up. Driving out of the pass through the Aures Mountains, the road flattens out, and groves of palm trees seem to spring up out of the sands. This area has many water wells, streams and river crossings.

After a few hours of driving the sun glides overhead taking the chill from the morning. Some sections of the road disappear under the shifting sands. The Citroën has no trouble going through; the rubber tracks effortlessly grip the loose sand.

Reggie stops the truck by an oasis. "Let's have some lunch, Jonesy. We should top up the petrol tank. The old girl uses more petrol than I thought she would. Our modifications to the engine do make her faster but we're going to pay for it in mileage I'm afraid."

"It's not all that bad Reg. With the bigger petrol tanks, and the extra gas cans, we've got plenty of range. I quite like the idea we've got the fastest thing going. I don't see anything but an airplane that can cross the desert as fast as we can.

Clive spots a boy seated on a rug under the shade of a palm tree. "I'll going to get some dried dates from the boy at the stand over there."

Reggie looks around from the back of the truck. "Don't gobble them all up. Remember the last time. You had gas for a week."

After they eat their lunch and top up the gas tank, Clive takes a turn driving. He is still popping dates in his mouth driving away from the oasis.

Reggie settles back in the passenger seat looking over a map. Wrinkling his nose, he lowers the map and looks over at Clive.

"How many of those things have you eaten? If we could bottle that we'd have enough gas to drive forever. Please have some mercy and put those blasted dates away."

Clive with one halfway to his mouth puts the date back and looks sheepishly at Reggie. "Sorry old sport, must have stepped in some camel dung."

Clive drives his three-hour shift and Reggie takes his turn behind the wheel.

"We're making good time. Why don't we just motor on in to Touggourt for dinner?"

"Sounds good to me Reg. I'd love a jolly good pint o' stout."

"Okay we'll stop up ahead for a minute. I need to put the antenna up and contact our man in Touggourt."

It is just getting dark when they pull up in front of a whitewashed building that is their grand European-style hotel. An ambitious French shipping conglomerate built hotels all across Algeria that are first rate in every respect. The architecture is a blend of native architecture, but on a larger scale. It features a squared façade with flat roofs, and multiple arched entrance ways. On one end is a domed structure that houses a theater. Inside the rooms all have a network of ceiling fans. Even in the winter months, the polished wood blades slowly revolve to keep the air moving.

The spacious lobby walls have framed paintings of desert scenes. The largest painting is on the wall behind the reception desk and depicts a camel caravan: a long line of the animals each packed with a heavy load of goods, silhouetted against a vivid blue sky, trekking atop the peaks of endless sand dunes.

Many of the floors are in a cool, polished stone, some with colorful patterns. Brightly colored Berber rugs are situated under carved wooden tables and wicker-backed chairs.

Clive stands behind Reggie at the reception desk, fiercely honking his nose into a handkerchief. Reggie, glancing back at Clive as he signs the register, says, "We'll need two rooms, hang the expense."

Clive looks up from inspecting his handkerchief. "You'll dash my spirit, old man. A good blow clears the head and cleanses the soul."

Reggie steps aside to let Clive sign in. "No offense, old sport, but a good night's sleep will keep my soul intact."

The man behind the reception desk hands Reggie an envelope. "A message for you, monsieur."

Reggie opens the envelope, reads the message and says to Clive, "It seems, Jonesy old sport, that S's man would like to buy dinner for us after we clean up. He says he would like to get off to a good start with us."

"I say, old top, so good to know we're wanted."

Reggie and Clive enter the dining room dressed for dinner. A man dressed in a sports coat over a roll top pullover greets them.

"My name is Jenson Clarkson. I'm pleased to meet the both of you. I have a table reserved."

Jenson leads them to the table. "Please be seated gentlemen. How about a drink to wash down this deuced sand?"

He signals a waiter to take their order.

"I hope that we can bring this op to a quick end. I hate this place. S wants you to take a tour of the desert below Ouargla, do your radio reports, and clear out. That way it's no trouble for you and S can get his team on the spot. We can all get back to merry old with the shine still on."

The waiter sits three pints of beer on the table and hands the trio menus. Clarkson picks up his beer, raises it in mock salute, and drains the glass.

Clive with some admiration quaffs half of his beer. Wiping the foam from his lip he says, "I say old man, that's quite a trick."

"No trick old fellow, drink is all I have to keep me company in this wretched hell hole."

Reggie sets the dimpled glass on the table. Turning the glass under the handle with his palms, he looks at Clarkson who is trying to get the waiter's attention to order another beer. "We are here to do a job for the Prime Minister, not S. It is important to me, and to our country, to find our quarry and do the job right. I don't think this is the place to discuss our business."

"S told me you're a right bastard. He said you'd try to do it your own way. Well no matter. He's sending Claire Fairthorpe to sort you out. She won't waste time with you. It means that I have to stick while you play out your bloody follies."

BOBO'S RAID

With the last exclamation Clarkson drains his second beer, and smacks the glass on the table. The other diners are taking notice of the loud voice Clarkson has taken on. Clarkson is either unaware or uncaring. He yells for the waiter to bring him another beer.

Reggie speaks in a calm voice trying to defuse the man's growing anger. "Tell me, while you can, about this Miss Fairthorpe. Is she to manage S's mission?"

"She's to sort you sport, and sort she will. Fairthorpe's S's top agent, the most loyal he has. The woman will do anything for his lordship. Claire always gets what she's after and never fails. If she can't tame you, she'll shoot you dead, you can be sure of that. I expect her in two or three days. S was sure you wouldn't play it his way. You'll stay here until she takes over."

"Thanks for the warning," Reggie says. "We'll be on our way in the morning."

Clarkson rises from the table and steadies himself with the back of his chair.

"You won't be going nowhere, sport. I've had coupl'a local boys take your Citroën for a ride. By the time they finish with it, I doubt it'll be fit for scrap. Dinner and the jokes on you, old sod."

With too much drink in him, Clarkson misses setting the empty beer glass back on the table. The empty glass crashes to the floor sending out shards under neighboring tables. He does not seem to notice, but wobbles unsteadily out of the room to the stares of startled diners.

Chapter 13

While waiters scurry to sweep up the broken glass, Clive and Reggie stand back from the broom handles poking back and forth around their table. Clive holding the beer mug close to his chest asks, "How did they find the truck?"

"I don't see how they could," Reggie replies. "I think Mr. Clarkson had too much to drink before we got here. What he did was give away his grand scheme. When I radioed our man Mays, he warned me to hide the truck when we got here. That's why we drove around to find the place. He must have known that Clarkson was up to something.

"With the battery and fuel cut-out switches we put in, no one can start it anyway. I didn't see any vehicle in this place that would be capable of towing it either."

The men take their seats after the waiters finish sweeping up. The patrons at the nearby tables moved to other tables farther away.

A man with a black beard, wearing a dark turban stops at the table.

"Good evening gentlemen, I take it you're new in town. Are you Mr. Bobrowski and Mr. Parry-Jones? I'm Terry Mays."

Reggie rises out of his chair to shake hands with Mays. "Nice to meet you, Mr. Mays, I'm Reggie and my friend is Clive or Jonesy as I tend to call him."

BOBO'S RAID

Clive reaches across the table to shake May's hand. "Jonesy is fine by me, Mr. Mays."

"Please, Terry's my name, nice to meet both of you. The Prime Minister tells me to take good care of you fellows."

"Please have a seat, Terry, welcome aboard. Thanks for warning us about Clarkson, he just left. He seems to be a man very unhappy with his lot in life. Before he stumbled away, he said that some locals would steal our truck and run it to scrap."

Mays pulls out a chair and sits across from Reggie and Clive. "The place I sent you to put your truck is safe. Clarkson will never find it. I don't think you two will be bothered by him much longer. Reports of his troubles with drink have gotten back to the home office. Claire Fairthorpe will be here soon. Rumor has it she has a replacement for him. She, by all accounts, is a beautiful but deadly lady. S, I'm told, is quite high on her. She's his main troubleshooter. I'm sure she'll want to take over your op."

Reggie signals a waiter. "We haven't had dinner yet, would you join us?"

Mays scans the room. "Yes please. I have information on the Germans' movements for you. I believe we are safe to talk here. I was sent here two years ago to do some work. I've traveled the country during the winter months so I can give you pointers on the lay of the land here."

"Are you from this part of the country?" asks Clive.

"No, my parents immigrated to England from India. In Arab countries my dark skin helps me blend in. When I'm wearing this beard and turban I can usually go about unnoticed. I do enjoy shaving the beard when I go home for a stay."

The men go silent as a waiter arrives to take their dinner order.

"You shouldn't have any trouble finding the German party; they are hovering about the Ouargla-Hassi Messaoud area and not making many friends. They have stolen sheep from the local Berbers down there. I learned from a merchant that the Germans depend on supplies coming from Algiers. When they run low, they try to buy from the locals. If the locals won't sell, they steal what they want.

"There are ten of them. Six of the men we don't have much information about. The main players are Viktor Nast, Eric Braun, Ernst Schulz, and Olaf Fischer.

"Viktor Nast is a university professor. He is a brilliant geologist and the main man in the search for oil. The vitals we have on him put him at 5'8" and 200 pounds. He is sixty years old, balding with white hair, and in good health.

"Eric Braun is the professor's assistant. Twenty four years old, 5'9", 165 pounds, light brown hair. He is a student of the professor and, we think, a capable man.

"Ernst Schulz is a major in the German army and the military officer in charge of the expedition. He is 5'10", 170 pounds, forty-eight years old, full head of dark brown hair. A career military man, not a Nazi party member as far as we can tell.

"The man to watch for is Olaf Fischer. Measures 6'0", 225 pounds, blond hair. He's a Nazi party man with a nasty criminal past. We can't find any military history for him. The thought from our men is that he is there to make sure the party is represented, oil is found, and to carry out any dirty work that becomes necessary.

"The other men are truck drivers and laborers. They have three Krupp semi-trucks. The drilling equipment demands the trucks have more carrying capacity than any half-track vehicles. My man here says the trucks get stuck in deep sand, much to the discontent of our German so-called archeologist friends.

The waiters bring trays of food to distribute around the table. Mays, with his dinner and tea set before him, looks longingly at the wine the others have with dinner. His Arab disguise means he must forgo spirits.

Reggie notes May's gaze. "I have an excellent bottle of brandy if you would care to join me in my room later. I'd like to jot down some of your information. Are the locals friendly in the areas we're going to?"

"I'll take you up on the brandy; the Berbers are friendly enough. There are bandits and cutthroats that roam about looking for easy prey. You know this is where Haardt and Audouin started the first of the Citroën expeditions. Twelve years ago they made it to Timbuktu in 20 days. They called their trucks caterpillar cars because of the endless belt tracks.

"The story goes they carried heavy machine guns on all of the trucks. I read that they set up demonstrations shooting the guns. The word spread quickly that they were not to be trifled with if you wanted to stay healthy."

Reggie nods in agreement. "I've read accounts of all of the Citroën expeditions I could find to this date. Very brave men, and great adventures. I tried to learn as much as possible from the articles. Clive and I gave this operation our utmost attention. We've made many modifications to our Citroën to make it faster, better handling, and to be as self-sufficient as possible.

"Let me assure you we are not unarmed. Clive has his Webley, I have my Colt. We have a compartment built into the floor of the truck with two Thompson submachine guns and two scoped Mauser rifles. Among the modifications we carried out is some light armor plating to the cab and rear cabin. The cabin ventilators swing out to act as gun ports. We can put up enough of a fight to discourage bandits."

After dinner, the men move to Reggie's room. Reggie pours three glasses of brandy. He writes in his journal as Mays recounts his information about the Germans.

Mays rolls his glass between his hands. "This is excellent brandy. It's been a while since I enjoyed a drink. Do either of you know about the oil discovery business?"

Reggie finishes writing in his journal. "I have friends in the oil business in America. I talked with them about what to look for. There are some clues in the land, but as they say in America, if want oil, you gotta drill for it."

Mays sips the last of his brandy. "Jolly good that, thanks gents. Our German friends have drilled the sands with no joy so I'm told. They do cover some territory circling Ouargla."

Reggie caps the brandy and hands the bottle to Mays, who bends in an elaborate bow. "I've got more in the truck, do enjoy yourself. I hope our work won't keep us from a bit of a dram now and again.

"We know," Reggie continues, "there is a large aquifer in that part of the Sahara, and that the water closest to the surface is salt-bearing. From what my oil men tell me there is a good chance of oil in the region. We're going to run out of winter soon and I want to locate the Germans as soon as possible. I think the best thing for Clive and me is to be on our way first light tomorrow. If Miss Fairthorpe wants to run this op, she'll have to find us first.

"I'll radio you when we get set up. The PM ordered this to be our mission, and to report to him through you. I don't want any interference from S or his minions."

Mays tucks the brandy bottle under his robes. "Good luck, old man. I won't give away any more than I have to, but I will have to work with Fairthorpe, whether I like it or not. If you have a message for the PM's ears only, open with the date and time. If the message is for all ears, open with time then the date, okay?"

"I understand," Reggie replies. "I may be rather vague as to our locations."

Terry Mays pauses at the door. "Stay clear of marauders: shoot first, don't wait for friendly declarations. Life is cheap here, like all the dark places on this earth. Mind Clarkson's men don't come after you in the morning. He may have posted watchers."

Chapter 14

"I say Reggie, I think we're being followed."

Up in the predawn darkness, the men are on their way out of the hotel. Light spills out from the hotel revealing the courtyard's frost-covered ground, their breath visible in the morning's chill. Creeping under the pillared archways they stay in the shadows. Once clear of the hotel, the alleys are dark save for the dim light of a crescent moon.

Not more than a hundred yards into their trip to the Citroën, Reggie stops and listens. He turns to Clive's dark outline and nods in agreement. Motioning for Clive to turn into the next alley he follows him in. They walk quietly to the next alley and turn again. They can hear the footsteps follow them with each turn.

"Right you are, Jonesy," Reggie whispers, "can you tell how many there are?"

"Certainly more than one, but I can't tell beyond that. Do you want to split up and see if we can shake them off?"

"No, we stay together. We don't know how many there are. I don't want us to get lost in these alleys. I'm going to have to go back toward the hotel to get my bearings as it is.

"Get your Webley out, go down the alley, and stay in the shadows. Talk to me in a low voice so they think I'm still beside you. I'll duck into the next doorway and get behind them. After you get to a place that's good and dark, see if you can surprise the front man. Go far enough so I get behind them...twenty yards or so.

"I'll try to take out the men in the rear as quietly as possible. I don't know who these guys are or why they're following us. We need to get to the truck and be on our way."

Clive nods in agreement, drawing his pistol as he continues down the alley.

Reggie slips into a deep-gated archway and presses his back to the rough wall. He can hear Clive's whispering voice fading in the stillness. Two men in Arab robes pass the archway a short time after Clive and Reggie parted. One of the Arabs pauses and looks directly at Reggie.

Reggie, staying stone-still, holds his breath. The Arab, not seeing any movement in the archway's darkness, moves on behind his companion. Reggie lets his breath out silently and steps from the archway. From what he can see the Arab in front is closing on Clive. The man in the rear checks each doorway before moving on. The distance grows between the two Arabs.

Reggie moves down the alley behind the men as quietly as he can. As he closes up on the second Arab, his foot scrapes across some gravel. He darts into a shallow doorway as the Arab turns back toward him. The Arab draws a long curved blade, holding it out in front of him. Moving with caution, the man hunts for the source of the noise.

Reggie crouches in the doorway; the Arab looks to his left at eye level, then to his right. Reggie springs, knocking the man down, then grabs the wrist of the man's hand holding the knife. They wrestle briefly before Reggie brings the butt of his Colt pistol down on the man's head.

The Arab following Clive hears the commotion, draws his blade and turns back.

Clive turns also; raising his pistol, he starts after the Arab. The man instantly turns, and rushes Clive. The blade flashes in the dull light as he slashes at Clive's head. Clive stumbles backward to ward off the vicious slashes of the wicked blade. The big Arab delivers a powerful blow that knocks the pistol from Clive's grasp. The Arab hears the pistol clatter to the ground and is on him at once. Clive grabs at the man's knife arm.

Reggie goes through the robes of the Arab he downed, trying to find some identification. He hears the struggle down the alley and runs toward his friend. Clive, on his back, holds the Arab's knife hand with both of his. The Arab punches at Clive's head with his other fist.

Reggie brings his Colt down on the Arab's head. The man continues to punch at Clive while twisting his head around to find his new attacker. Reggie yanks the turban off the big Arab's head and clubs him with all his strength.

Clive pushes the Arab off him and scrambles to his knees as Reggie helps him to his feet.

"I owe you that one, Reg. He knocked the pistol out of my hand. I'm bloody lucky he didn't cut off my wrist. Thought I was a goner."

Reggie hands Clive his scarred Webley. "That guy is built like a gorilla. Let's not waste any time. We need to get on the way.

BOBO'S RAID

I didn't find anything on the other guy so we're no closer to knowing who they are. Grab his knife; it may tell us something."

Clive looks up at the skyline. "I think I remember the outline of that Mosque. I'm sure the Citroën's just a block over."

Reggie looks up too. "I hope you're right."

A short time later the Citroën rolls down the road toward Ouargla. The rubber caterpillar tracks create large footprints that glide over the dusty road, humming with an endless vibration.

Clive rummages in his rucksack mumbling, "I can't find my cheaters; the bloody sun is blistering my eyeballs."

Reggie has his dark glasses on, his cap pulled down over his brow. "I'm afraid I wasn't keeping watch the last time you wore them. Was it my turn to keep track of your wardrobe?"

"Very funny that. If you can keep this thing from jostling about, I'll go in back to see if I can find them."

"Here, you can wear my cap till we stop for lunch."

"I'd rather blister my eyeballs than wear that silly cap, old man. I'll risk the back."

Reggie shrugs, "It's the latest fashion in Florida golf caps."

Clive does an elaborate roll of his eyes. "It's no small wonder the colonials are thought of as heathens."

The road is well-marked. The Citroën eats the distance to Ouargla at 40 kilometers an hour. Water sluices down the irrigation canals near by.

Off in the distance the sand dunes are pink against a vivid blue sky. Thick patches of agriculture with hundreds of palm trees are surrounded by desert sands.

To Reggie, almost hypnotized by the tracks in the sand, it seems strange that acres of green growing vegetation are in the midst of such an arid landscape.

The sprawling city of Ouargla becomes visible to the west. Reggie drives through narrow streets to a modern hotel. The Europa is on the south end of the city. The building is styled after a Moorish castle, with a light rose-colored exterior and elaborate archways.

Inside the hotel, the front desk is a dark, almost black, wood. The top has inlaid tiles in blue and gold. The long counter is bordered with a highly polished brass rail.

Reggie, followed by Clive, puts his bag down in front of the desk to check in. "Good afternoon, we'd like two rooms please."

The man behind the counter answers in English with a heavy French accent.

"We 'ave the rooms front and back, you know."

"Is someone on duty here at night?" Reggie asks.

"Oui, monsieur, we staff all the night."

Reggie puts his passport on the counter. "We ran into some bandits in Touggourt. I'd like our rooms to be in sight of your management day and night. I also need a place to secure our vehicle. We have a special Citroën that bandits would find valuable. Do you know of a place nearby?"

"Oui, the gendarmerie is two of the doors away. They have the place to lodge the autos. I can call to make for you to place the Citroën."

Reggie picks up the pen to sign hotel's register. "Please do, I'll feel much better knowing we, and the vehicle, are safe from scoundrels."

BOBO'S RAID

The man behind the counter, the phone receiver to his ear, pulls the register away. He holds up one finger in indication to wait. His conversation on the phone is brief.

"Monsieur, the Capitaine asks to speak with you. You are to go to him with your passports."

Chapter 15

Going the "two doors down" is a long way after walking past a block of the hotel's frontage. A French tricolor flag hangs above the door. Clive and Reggie go though the open door to find a uniformed officer slouched behind a scarred wooden counter. The officer raises his head. Looking them up and down, he asks gruffly, "Qu'est-ce que vous voulez?" (What do you want?)

Reggie is trying to decipher the question when a voice from a rear office commands, "Envoyez-les moi (Send them to me)." The officer opens a gate and motions for the men to go though.

Sitting in a swivel chair is a heavyset man, his scalp pink, ringed with dark hair. The hair is creased where his traditional police hat is usually worn. He is leaning back, hands behind his head, with a black cigar in his mouth. The end is aglow, filling the room with acrid smoke, the smell akin to burning dung.

The man leans forward in his chair. "Bon jour messieurs. Parly French?"

Reggie pulls his cap off and steps forward. "My French is terrible I'm afraid."

"No matter," the man says. "My English is good. You are the men sent from the hotel?"

"Yes sir, we are looking for a safe place to put our Citroën for the night."

BOBO'S RAID

"Let me see your passports."

The men step forward and place their passports on the well-kept desk.

The man in the chair picks up each passport; he studies the pictures for several minutes. He looks up from the passports to scrutinize each man's face. After going through the pages, he leans back in the chair putting the papers down close to him.

"I am Captain Lom. My question to you is, are you here to bring trouble to my little slice of heaven?"

Reggie and Clive both answer "No" at the same time.

Reggie says "Let me explain, Captain."

The captain flicks the ash from his cigar, holds up his hand, palm out. "What I want to know is why you are here, and why you need my protection."

"There seems to be some misunderstanding," Reggie says. "I did not ask for your protection sir. I simply wanted a secure place to leave the Citroën while we are here."

"What is your business here?" Reaching down Lom flips open Reggie's passport. "Mr. Bobrowski."

"Clive and I have modified our Citroën for the desert. We're here to test our work. We are also looking into the feasibility of extending the railroad system."

The captain sits forward in his chair. "Your Citroën, it is one of the caterpillar cars?"

"Yes, but quite a bit different from the ones that came through here in 1922."

"I have made requests for one every year I have been stationed here. Do you think my high and mighty superiors would listen?

Non, non, why should I have such a thing? Camels, mules, old Ford cars, that is fitting for this place.

"Before I come to see your special Citroën, and you buy a cognac, I tell you I will not have you make trouble here. The Boche are trouble enough. Any more of the problems with the Berbers and there will be the uprising."

"I will be pleased to buy the cognac, captain," Reggie says. "We are not here to make trouble. This trip for us is more of an escape from the English winter, having some fun driving in the desert. We hope to persuade some army types to buy our modified Citroëns. I believe the possibility of extending rail service would only be feasible if the country is at peace."

Captain Lom puts on his uniform coat and hat. "Come gentlemen, some small refreshment is needed to begin the evening."

Picking up the passports from his desk, Lom returns them on his way to the door.

Lom, leading the men walking at a fast pace, rounds the wall at the driveway to the hotel. The Citroën parked in front of the hotel has a crowd of men and boys around it. A man, with his hands pressed against the passenger window shading his eyes, is trying to get a look inside.

Lom shouts, "Allez-vous!" He waves his arms in a shooing motion. The crowd reluctantly moves away as the captain gets closer. Going directly to the tracks, Lom runs his hands over the rubber ribs. He pulls at the raised ribs that grip the sand trying to gauge its stiffness.

BOBO'S RAID

Reggie and Clive look on fascinated by this action. People from everywhere they have been with the Citroën do almost the same thing. The tracks, more than any other feature of the truck, are the first thing that piques curiosity. Lom tries the door handle. "Well, open it up. I must see the insides."

Clive opens the passenger side door to let Lom have a look inside. Members of the remaining crowd push forward to get a look.

Reggie quickly opens the driver's door. "Jump in captain. We'll take you for a ride."

Clive gets in hunched behind the passenger seat, then he motions the captain to step up and sit in the seat.

Reggie starts the engine. Using the horn, he drives slowly through the gathering out of the hotel's gravel lot.

"I'd rather not have too much of our wares shown off. We've some valuables aboard that might attract the wrong sort of interest."

Lom, swiveling his head looking about the cabin asks, "Tell me what is so special about your caterpillar? I have not been inside one of these. I read the many adventures of Messieurs Haardt and Audouin as soon as they are published. Great men of France. André Citroën, I think is a great man."

Clive, crouching behind the seats, begins a description of the modifications he helped carry out.

"This is one of the first fully-enclosed extended cabs. We had our own coach-maker do the work. We extended the frame for a longer wheelbase to give us more room in the rear compartment. Reggie and I did the engine work: it's a 3.5 liter six-cylinder that has more power and torque than any other Citroën. We put in a five-speed transmission which was a lot of work, but it gives us better top speed. We've done over 40 miles an hour on tarmac. We had to make a new tensioning system for the tracks to keep them on at that speed.

"The drive is on the forward end of the track now; we mounted it on our own flexible mounts for better traction and a smoother ride."

Reggie, driving through the narrow streets, uses the horn to move through throngs of people and animals.

"When we come to the outskirts of town, captain, I'll stop so we can show you the back compartment."

They drive out of the streets to the end of town. Hundreds of date palm trees range to the east. Reggie stops, shuts off the engine and climbs out of the door. The captain goes out of his door followed by Clive. Reggie opens the rear door to pull down a hinged ladder used to climb into the rear compartment.

After the captain climbs in, Reggie explains, "This is our home while we are in the desert. We keep food and water in the racks on the sides. Our bunks fold up against the sides. The radios are on the table at the front. They are the latest aircraft types; we can talk with our wives in England."

Lom goes to the radios, closely inspecting the dials and wheels. "Mon Dieu, you speak to England on these little sets? I should have such a magnificent carriage to hunt down the heathens that cause me so many sleepless nights."

Reggie folds down a small table, removes a bottle of cognac from a shelf, and pours three glasses. "I didn't forget the cognac I promised. I think you can see why we would like some place safe to park the vehicle."

Lom sips from his glass. "You can be sure your caterpillar will be safe with me, messieurs."

Reggie holds out his keys. "Would you care to drive us back to town, captain?"

Lom raises his brow in a quizzical look to see if Reggie is having a joke on him. Not one to hesitate, he snatches the keys as he goes out the back of the truck.

By the time Reggie and Clive close up the rear door and get to the front, the captain has the engine started. He is studying the gauges as the men scramble in.

Lom, having watched Reggie drive, finds first gear; releasing the clutch, the Citroën moves off smoothly. The captain looks over at Reggie with a wide grin on his face. Reggie returns the grin with a thumbs up. They make a wide turn to head back into the city.

Lom, not using the track steering system, makes slow wide turns through the narrow alleys. Holding down the horn button, he motors past startled tradesmen. The unlit cigar clamped in his teeth cannot hide the wide smile on the captain's face. He waves his arm out of the window to the people in the streets.

They pull into a gated archway by the police station, back to a lot with an ancient Ford car and horse-drawn carts. Reggie shows Lom how to engage the tracks' turning system. Lom takes some time to understand, then pivots the truck on a stopped track to face the archway.

Lom steps from the truck and pats the fender. "Tres magnifique. What a vehicle." He hands the keys to Reggie.

"Will you join us for a drink in the hotel, captain?"

"Merci, but of course, I will join you at the hotel. I enjoyed very much the driving, mes amis. This is a day I will long remember. If you will lead, I will lock the gate after you."

Reggie and Clive check into the hotel. After a quick wash up they head downstairs. Crossing the foyer to the entrance of the restaurant, they hear Captain Lom recounting his adventure with the Citroën. He is sitting on a bar stool with his back to the bar. The glass of wine in his hand is in danger of spilling as he waves his arm in demonstration of driving the truck.

"Ah, welcome, mes amis. I was just explaining the skills required to drive the caterpillar. Come, we will sit at the table."

The captain leads the men to a table in a far corner away from other diners.

"I have ordered a very nice bottle of Burgundy from a district not far from my home in France."

A waiter arrives at the table to pop the cork from the bottle with a practiced flourish. Lom examines the bottle, waves away the waiter, and pours three glasses himself.

Lom raises his glass. "To a pleasant, and I hope trouble free, excursion for my new friends."

Reggie raises his glass in salute. "How long have you been stationed here, captain?"

"It will be five years this July. I feel it is a lifetime of heat and trouble. I wonder if it is a penance for some sin I committed. I met my wife in this country, and for that I am grateful."

BOBO'S RAID

Grimacing, Clive sets down his glass. "I'm really more a bitters man." Clearing his throat, he asks. "What sort of troubles do you have here, captain?"

"We have the usual thievery, bandits, and murder. Things can become serious if the natives think a crime is committed against their religion. A major uprising comes like a sand storm if I cannot make the peace.

"The Boche bring me trouble: they steal from the Berbers, and now it seems one of the young girls has gone missing. One of the Germans is a brute, Olaf he is called. He will add to my troubles and yours also if you run into him.

"I must be off. My wife will be waiting supper for me. I will have the gate open by 7:30. Thank you for the wine."

Lom returns the cork, winks with a smile, and takes the bottle with him.

Chapter 16

Having enjoyed a good night's sleep in a comfortable bed, Reggie and Clive order a big breakfast in the restaurant. Taking time to savor the fresh eggs and excellent coffee, Reggie drinks the last of his coffee and looks at his watch.

"That should give the captain plenty of time to unlock the gate for us." Reggie puts his napkin on the table and asks Clive, "Are you ready to go?"

Clive, mopping up the egg yoke with the last piece of bread, nods to confirm.

Walking to the police station, they see Captain Lom outside the police station in an animated conversation with a small group of men. The native men are waving their arms, making figures and gestures with their hands, trying to overcome the language barrier.

Lom nods his head, agreeing to the gestures. He shakes each man's hand. "I will send my men to help you find your goats. Understand?"

One of the men is translating; the others look to him and back to the captain. They bow, and move away talking amongst themselves.

Lom turns to go into the station when he sees Reggie and Clive.

"Bon jour mes amis, you are ready for the Citroën?"

BOBO'S RAID

"Good morning captain. Yes, we are eager to test the worst of the desert. Were those Tuareg men you were talking to?"

"Oui, but I still know little of their language. There are too many dialects for me to understand. Someone has run off their goat herds. They want the Boche to pay for the goats. I do not know if the Germans are responsible.

"These people depend on their herds of goats for food and clothing. Life here is held by a thin thread. I do not think the Germans care. I fear these people who are poor, but very proud, will look for the revenge.

"If they are to attack the Germans they will be killed. If this is to happen there will be much blood spilled. Many of the Berber people will join to fight. The Germans will not be the only white men to die."

Captain Lom walks to the gate of the police lot with Reggie and Clive in tow. He unlocks the gate and goes with them to the Citroën.

"My advice is for you to go to the south; you will find deep sand and difficult terrain. Surely this will be enough of the difficulties to test the worth of your caterpillar. The Boche are somewhere to the east. This is an area you should avoid. I must send some of my men today to locate them. I promised to put an end to the Germans raiding the Berbers.

"If I cannot put an end to this, I will have to call in the Army. There is much what you call the bad blood between the Legionaires and the Berbers."

Reggie and Clive shake the captain's hand.

"Thanks for your help, captain."

"You will report to me should you find the Germans. I want to have you in good health. We can share much of your good brandy, mes amis."

Reggie and Clive check over the Citroën, before starting the engine to give it a brief warm up. They drive away, kicking up dust and sand.

"So, Reg old man, just where are we headed?"

"We're going to go south as the captain said for a while. I have an idea he may be keeping an eye on us. He may seem the backwoods cop, but I think he may be the clever lad. We'll go a few miles and turn east. I'm anxious to find our German friends. That was the purpose as I remember. It seems a donkey's age since we started this trip."

After turning to the east, the drive toward Hassi Messaoud is dusty but not unpleasant. The morning is warm, not yet hot. Reggie drives the Citroën up a high dune to survey the countryside. Taking his field glasses, he looks for any sign of the German party or recent tire tracks.

The sands are seemingly endless. There are small patches of green, not the palm trees of an oasis. The patches, spaced far apart, and irregularly, are shrubs struggling to claw their way above the suffocating sands.

Clive climbs from the truck, stretches, arching his back with a moan. He retrieves a telescope from the Citroën, fits it to his eye and scans to the south. The dunes conceal any form of life. Clive soon tires of sighting through the glass. As he turns from the south a movement catches his eye. Focusing in, he sees a small group of people waving their arms over what seems to be a hole in the sand.

BOBO'S RAID

Reggie is scanning to the east when Clive nudges his arm. "Take a look over here. What do you make of that, old man?"

Clive points to the place he saw the group of people. Reggie scans in the direction of Clive's pointing. At first he sees nothing but sand, then a flash of sunlight catches his focus. He and Clive zero in on the group with their eyepieces. The puzzle becomes clearer when they both see spurts of sand thrown from the hole.

Reggie lowers the binoculars to try to judge the distance to the group. "I think someone is down in that hole trying to get out, or trying to get something out. Let's go see if we can help."

Piling into the Citroën, the men, released from boredom, race over the dunes to the group gathered around the hole. As the truck nears they can see two women and four children in a state of agitation. Two dogs are running around the perimeter of the hole, barking.

Reggie and Clive stop the truck yards from the group, trying to ascertain the commotion. An older woman breaks from the group and runs toward the Citroën waving her arms. When Reggie climbs out, the women tugs at his arm pointing to the hole. He looks over at Clive as he gets out of the truck. They both run to the hole.

Two boys and a man are in the hole. The boys are trying to scoop sand out of the hole with their hands. The man is buried to his chin. He has one hand out of the sand fanning it away from his face. Sand is shifting back into the hole as fast as the boys can throw it out. The boys are now in danger of being buried also.

"Clive, get back in the truck. I'm going to get a rope and tie it off to it. You get ready to back up when I signal."

Reggie pulls a coil of rope from inside the truck. He ties one end to the front tow hook on the Citroën, and runs back to the hole letting the rope uncoil.

He throws the rope to the boys in the hole and pantomimes putting the rope under the arms of the man. One of the boys grabs the rope but looks back at Reggie in confusion. Reggie takes the slack in the rope and wraps it under his arms. He points to the man in the hole.

In his frustration he yells, "Put it under his arms, boy! Hurry, you'll all go under."

The other boy in the hole grabs the rope; he loops it over the man's head trying to get it under his hand. The man takes the rope in his hand. Reggie motions for the boys to grab the rope too. The sand is filling the hole.

"Back it up Jonesy. Go slow; don't pull it out of their hands. Go slow."

Reggie lifts the rope to show Clive the slack. The rope pulls taut.

Reggie tries to get the two boys to climb up the rope. The women are screaming, dogs are barking, and sand is filling the hole. The boys are terrified and confused. Reggie, unable to communicate, grows desperate to get them out. He yells to Clive to stop the truck.

"Clive, stop the truck and help me!"

Clive throws the gear lever into neutral and jumps from the truck, running to Reggie.

"Hold on to my legs, I'm going to get the boys out."

BOBO'S RAID

Going down on his knees, Reggie edges to the hole with Clive holding on to his ankles. Following the rope to reach the first boy, he grabs the boy's arm and yells for Clive to pull them up. As soon as the boy is in reach, the two women haul him up past Reggie.

Reggie goes headfirst back into the hole reaching out for the second boy, but the boy is holding the rope with both hands, sand cascading over his face. Reggie, pulls himself down on the rope, trying to pry the boy's hands from the rope. He is pulling Clive into the hole with him. Reggie, with his belly in the sand, has one hand on the boy's arm. He arches his back and slaps the boy's head with his right hand.

The panic-stricken boy lets go of the rope. "Pull us up! Pull, pull!" Reggie yells.

Clive, lying on his belly hauls back on Reggie's legs. He struggles with the weight. Up on his knees, then his on back, he pulls them to the surface. The women grab at the boy who is sobbing uncontrollably.

Reggie, peering back down the hole, sees only the hand of man clutching the rope in the hole. Sand covers his head.

"Clive I'm going back for the guy. I'm going to try and get the rope under his arms. Give me some slack in the rope. When I kick my feet, jump in the truck and pull us out. You can't pull our weight with all that sand; you've got to use the truck. Go slow, we don't want to cut the man in half."

Before Clive can argue the point, Reggie flops over the edge of the hole.

Chapter 17

The sand, warm and loose, slowly cascades down the sides of the hole. Reggie uses the rope to scale downward, the coarse sand rushes up his pant legs. The man in the hole is shaking his head violently trying to keep the sand from completely burying him. Squeezing the man's outreached hand reassuringly, Reggie paddles furiously to get the sand away from the man's face.

Taking the rope, Reggie digs into the sand and manages to get it under one arm. Paddling the sand again, he pulls the rope under the other arm and around the man's back. Knotting the rope, he kicks his feet signaling Clive to haul away. As soon as the rope pulls taut, he starts scooping the sand away from the man's body.

The man groans as the rope pulls against the sand's grip. Reggie manages to free both of the man's arms, paddling the sand away. He knows the strain of the rope must be terrible, but there is nothing else he can do. The man's body is slowly coming out of the sand. Reggie now has to hold onto the rope with one hand. He uses his left hand to continue to scoop the sand away.

After the man's waist clears the sand, the rope snatches both men from the hole. The women wail and run to the dark-skinned man. Reggie turns the man over to unknot the rope. Turning the man's head he listens for breathing. With an open palm, Reggie pounds the man's back until, with a cough, he spews sand, followed by a deep gasp.

The younger woman kneels by the gasping man. Cooing softly she pulls his head to her lap. She tenderly wipes sand from his face, and pours some water from a goat skin on his mouth. She looks up at Reggie, tears running down her cheeks. "Merci, merci beaucoup."

The two boys with the older woman gather to look down on the prone man. The small boy is still knuckling his red eyes.

"De rien," Reggie replies.

Clive nudges Reggie with a water canteen. Reggie takes a drink, washes it around in his mouth, and spits out water and sand. He takes another long drink and swallows.

Reggie points to the depression in the sand. "What happened?"

The women shrug their shoulders. Reggie walks to the edge of the almost filled in hole and points again. He turns back to the women with his arms up, hands inverted, palms out.

The face of the older woman brightens. "Hassi, hassi." She makes a motion with her hands of digging. The younger woman says "Puits, le puits."

Reggie looks to Clive, "He was digging a well."

Clive shakes his head. "A well in the middle of the bloody desert? He must be daft."

"Maybe not, Jonesy. There is an aquifer under all this. No one knows how big it is. He was digging by those shrubs; they get water to their roots somehow. Whatever he was shoring up the hole with must have collapsed. Let's go back to the hotel and get cleaned up.

We'll have a good dinner; tomorrow I'll ask Lom where we can get some stone and mortar."

Clive sits on the fender of the Citroën shaking sand from his shoe. "We're well diggers then, are we?"

Reggie swats at the sand on his shirt and pants. "We can use the exercise. Besides, if we don't help, I'd be willing to wager the guy will be back at it. I'd hate to see him lose his whole family under the sand. If there is water, he'll be the local king of the dunes."

Reggie climbs behind the steering wheel of the Citroën, and turns around to head back to Ouargla.

"I keep thinking how lucky we are not to be freezing our backsides back home. The warm sun's a treat, but I have to tell you, I really hate sand in my underwear."

Clive looks over at Reggie studying his face to see if he was serious. He bursts out with a huge laugh. "You bloody great fool. You damned near took us both to the bottom of the Sahara. You jumped into that sand pit head first. What in the name of heaven were you thinking? Sand in your underwear! You twit, you're lucky to be feeling the bloody sand."

"Jonesy old man, don't look now, someone might think you care. You know if I had thought about what might have happened, I probably wouldn't have done it."

"No, you'd've still done it. I'm tryin' to tell you, you're damned lucky to be feelin' sand, that's all."

"You've never hesitated to stand in old friend; you're one in a million, mate. But, all in all, the sand's still grating my bum."

Back at the hotel after washing away the sand, Reggie and Clive go the bar to find Captain Lom sitting by himself at a table.

"Ah, mes amis. The heroes of the desert have returned. Come join me please."

The men take seats at the captain's table.

"You may have... how you say, save my bacon. The jungles drums are beating the praises of your daring rescue. The Berbers are tres happy."

Reggie trades a look of surprise with Jonesy. "Does news always travel this fast?"

"Non, one of my patrols just returned with the happy news. I feel we should celebrate. Perhaps a fine supper to have with your superb brandy."

Reggie throws his head back with a laugh. "Bien sur, mon capitaine."

"Did I get left out?"

"Why no Jonesy I wouldn't want you to feel left out. I just said that you'd be happy to buy the captain supper."

Reggie, expecting a whelp of indignation from Clive, sees his friend's face frozen in astonishment.

"My god Reg, I thought that was Ally for a minute. If she had blond hair... or I have been in the desert too long?"

A striking full-figured brunette, wearing a dark blouse and riding jodhpurs, locks eyes with Reggie. Her head tilts forward to walk with a very determined stride heading for their table.

The captain turns in his chair to see what the other men are seeing.

"Ah, the terrible Claire," he says.

When she recognizes Captain Lom, the woman's walk slows to become a more casual pace. She continues to the table.

"Hello, Lom."

"Bonjour, Mademoiselle Fairthorpe. You have returned to grace our troubled patch of sand."

"I will be staying for a time, captain. Who are your friends?"

"Forgive me; I thought you knew each other."

The captain looks for a reaction from Clive and Reggie.

Their faces show him nothing.

"May I present Count Bobrowski, and Clive Parry-Jones.

Gentlemen, this is Mademoiselle Claire Fairthorpe."

Reggie and Clive get up from of their chairs to greet Miss Fairthorpe. Captain Lom remains seated.

Claire Fairthorpe glares into Reggie's face with a ferocity matched only by her handshake. She waves away Clive's offered hand.

Reggie attempts some courtesy to defuse the awkward moment.

"Please have a seat. Will you have dinner with us?"

Claire glances down at Captain Lom. "I haven't time. I have been instructed by my office to see that you two do not get into any trouble while you are here on holiday. You will meet with me in my office tomorrow morning. I will list the places you can go, and what you should do while you are under my supervision."

Lom pours wine into his glass while watching Claire, with her hands on her hips, lean forward telling Reggie what she wants.

Reggie looks at Clive whose face is clouding, his eye lids narrowing. Lom smiles with a slight shake of his head.

Reggie flashes his best smile. "I'm terribly sorry, but we've a previous engagement."

Claire brushes back her the hair from her forehead, her jaw clinched. "A previous engagement? Doing what, larking about?"

"Excuse me Miss Fairthorpe, we seem to have gotten off to a bad start. Clive and I are here to work, we have a schedule. Tomorrow morning we will be working on a water well some miles from here. I do not feel any need to be under your supervision. I'm sure you have far more important things to do with your time. If you will excuse us, we are about to have supper with our friend here."

"Mind your friends…Bobo. I came today as a courtesy. When charged with an assignment, I do not fail."

She turns and walks away as quickly as she came.

Lom with a mischievous smile asks, "Bobo, you are a bobo?"

Clive laughs. "That's what Reggie's wife calls him. He doesn't like it."

Lom still smiling asks. "How is it the lovely Miss Fairthorpe calls you by this name?"

Before Clive can answer Reggie says, "Too many people know the name in England. It is an embarrassment. Your Miss Fairthorpe seems to enjoy setting the knife."

"Non, is not my Fairthorpe. It is said that her father was a spy for both the Germans and the British in the

Great War. She, I think, is a British agent who brings trouble to my little patch. Trouble I do not need."

Chapter 18

As it turns out, digging a well by hand is a lot of work. Reggie and Clive first erect a temporary barrier to keep the sand out of the hole. They drive iron pipes through the sand into the hard earth around the perimeter of the hole. After securing corrugated iron sheeting to the pipes, they run braces from the pipes to stakes pounded into solid ground.

Clearing sand out of the hole is easy. They find the hard earth below the sand too tough for shovels. In order to swing a pickax they have to move the sand barrier back. All of this is watched carefully by the two women and the two boys.

Later in the first day the dark man they rescued hobbles out to the hole. The younger woman keeps saying in broken French that the well is theirs.

Clive mopping the sweat from his eyes says, "What is she going on about, old boy?"

"I think she's saying the well belongs to them," Reggie replies. "I am trying to tell her we know that. I can't get it through to her. Let's go get lunch in town. I'll find someone who can speak the language and when we get back we'll find out what's going on."

On their return from lunch in Ouargla they bring a man from Lom's police unit. He follows behind in an old Ford car, jouncing over the rough terrain. Arriving back at the well they find the women trying to pull out the pipes they drove into the ground.

Clive jumps from the Citroën and rushes toward the well hole.

"Stop that you idiots. Do you think that's funny? Get away from the hole!"

The women shrink back from Clive. The husband hobbles out of the hut they call home with an ancient-looking long rifle.

The policeman, holding up his hands, steps between the man with the rifle and Clive. Speaking to the man with the rifle in a calm voice, the policeman uses language the rifleman apparently understands. As soon as the man lowers the rifle, the two women join in the arm-waving conversation.

The policeman motions Reggie and Clive to join him.

"Messieurs, the peoples are saying they are grateful for your saving the man and boys. They do not think you should take their well from them."

Clive blurts out, "Take their well!"

Reggie puts his hand on Clive's shoulder. "Take it easy, Jonesy. These people don't know us. Let's just let the policeman speak with them."

Reggie turns to the policeman. "Please tell them we are digging the well for them; we don't want their well for ourselves."

The policeman relays Reggie's message to the man and the two women. They talk amongst themselves, and then to the policeman.

"They want to know why you would do this."

Reggie says, "Please tell them we are afraid for them if they try to do it themselves. The boys might be hurt or someone killed. We would like to continue the dig to see if there is water. We do not want to annoy them, or control the well. This is a gesture of goodwill.

Clive and I will be traveling throughout the area to test our vehicle. We know the Germans have caused some bad feelings. It's our intention to show these people that we are their friends. We'll leave as soon as the well is finished."

The policeman relays Reggie's message. The Berbers hold a brief talk amongst themselves, and the man with the rifle speaks to the policeman.

The policeman turns to Reggie and Clive. "The man wants to thank you for saving him and his children. He asks that God protect you. He says he will soon be able to help you."

The younger woman leads her husband back into the hut. The older woman, still suspicious, glares at Clive and Reggie, then follows the others back into the hut.

Reggie presses a few coins in the policeman's palm and watches the old Ford kick up dust heading back to Ouargla.

Reggie takes a pickax from the Citroën. "Well, let's get to it, old son."

Clive grunts, and follows Reggie, dragging a shovel behind him.

The men build a rhythm digging and removing the dirt. In the next days they deepen the hole rapidly. When the man digging gets tired they trade places.

The husband tries to help but it is soon evident that he is getting in the way. He and the young boys begin doing their normal chores and stay out of the way.

Reggie helps Clive erect an A-frame over the hole to haul the dirt up. He and Clive can now raise and lower themselves to the depths of the hole.

The women attach rugs to cover the top of the A-frame to give shade to the diggers. Both of the women are now bringing out dates and water to the men. Clive smiles and winks at the older woman to lighten her mood toward them.

Reggie hauls up the basket to throw the dirt by the family's little vegetable garden. Lugging the basket to the pile he picks up a wooden rake to spread the dirt out. He stops raking and cocks his head at the sound of a familiar voice.

Clive's yells echo up from the hole. "Reg, hey Reggie, I've got mud on me bloody shovel. Hey Reg, can't you hear me?"

Reggie runs to the hole. "I hear you, old frog. Good job, throw the mud in the basket and keep digging."

Reggie hauls up the next basket heavy with mud. After two more baskets Clive calls out again.

"Reggie haul me up out of here; water's coming in fast."

Reggie pulls on the rope that slides through the sheaves of the compound pulley at the top of the A-frame. Clive scrambles from the well holding a basket that has water running through it.

The older woman coming from the hut puts down her dates and cups her hands under Clive's basket. Her eyes dance as she tastes the cool well water. She bows to Reggie and Clive then turns, prancing back to the hut, her high pitched voice signaling her delight.

BOBO'S RAID

"Well Jonesy, that pretty much says it all. Let's get our stuff and be on the way. I think we deserve the hotel's finest dinner tonight."

The lights in the hotel are on by the time they get back to Ouargla. Both men, tired from the days of digging, go to their rooms to shower. The cool shower restores their energy. They walk down the hallway heading for the restaurant. At the restaurant they see Captain Lom sitting alone at his table.

"Mind if we join you, captain?"

"Did you bring your brandy?" Lom asks.

Reggie grins. "No, but I think a bottle of good champagne is in order if that will do."

"Certainement, mes amis, please have a seat. You have good news for me?"

Clive pulls a chair out. "Take a seat, Reg, I'll get the champers."

Reggie sits down across from Lom. "Do you mean to tell me your desert grapevine hasn't already reported in? We struck water."

"Mon Dieu, a one in million chance. You have given the greatest gift those people could dream of."

"We did the digging but the guy that started the well was right on the money. It's a nice feeling to help them out. Finding water was the best we could hope for."

"I am surprised I did not get the word," Lom says. "The first bottle will be for me to buy. What is it you English say?" Lom looks out into space drumming his fingers on the table. A big grin spreads over his face. "Ah, it is, good on you mate. Non?"

"Spot on," Reggie says with a laugh. "Only one bottle tonight captain. More than that and I'll fall asleep at the table. Jonesy will testify that digging is hard work."

In the morning, Reggie stands in front of the mirror in his room in his undershirt and shorts wiping shaving cream from his face. The door to the room rattles with a hard pounding. He cracks open the door to see who is pounding. Claire Fairthorpe pushes the door open to enter the room. She turns with hands on hips. "Get your bloody clothes on, Bobrowski."

"Oh excuse me, Miss Fairthorpe. I wasn't expecting the pleasure of your visit. Would you like to wait outside while I dress?"

"Just get your pants on. I thought I made it clear that you were to follow the Germans. I find out that you've been digging a well for some bloody heathens out in the desert."

"I can see why you and S get on," Reggie grumbles. "You both lack any social manners. By the way, you are the heathen in this country."

"I don't care about this country," Claire angrily replies. "My mission is to see if the Germans find oil. If you can't get on with it, I'll go myself."

Buttoning his pants, Reggie shakes his head. "There is no word that the Germans have found anything. The Berbers keep track of them. After the Jerry's killed some of the Berbers' sheep, the Berber men keep watch. If you are so keen on finding them, go rent a camel and have at it."

"I won't need a camel. I'll have Mr. S commandeer your Citroën if you don't get a move on. When will you learn we mean business? I know dozens of men here that would gladly cut your throat."

"Thank you, Miss Fairthorpe. I will pass your message along to the PM. Now kindly get the hell out of my room."

Claire pushes by Reggie on her way out of the room. "Your title and money mean nothing here. The PM can't save you in this desert rat's nest. You are a poor choice for this job…Bobo."

She slams the door hard on her way out.

Chapter 19

Reggie finds Clive in the restaurant sitting at a table with plates filled with a huge English breakfast. Clive speaks with a mouthful of egg. "Grab a plate and have a seat, old goat. I ordered enough for both of us."

Rolling his eyes at the mountain of food, Reggie takes a seat.

Clive mischievously wiggles his eyebrows. "Did I just see your friend Claire leaving?"

Reggie spoons some eggs and sausage onto his plate. "My friend stopped by to issue an order. She says get on with it or she'll put one of dozens of men on to cut my throat. I don't think she likes me."

Clive puts down his tea cup. "I wonder what makes such a beautiful woman so nasty."

"I'll tell you Jonesy, I don't really want to know. But she's right about getting on with it. Let's get the Citroën from Lom, and see if we can find the Jerrys. It's time to take some action."

When Clive and Reggie enter the office, Captain Lom has his feet up on the desk. Hands behind his head, puffing on the first cigar of the day, he gazes into space.

Reggie raps on the door frame. "Sorry to disturb you captain. Looks like you have a lot on your mind."

Startled from his daydreams, the chair springs forward. Lom chuckles. "Oui, a hard job. There is much weight to carry. Are you off on another adventure with the Citroën caterpillar?"

"We are indeed," Reggie replies. "As soon as we resupply, we'll be off. We're planning to be gone for a least a week. The Citroën needs a long run over deep sand and rough terrain." Reggie holds up a brown bottle topped with a blue-waxed cork. "I brought you a bottle of brandy to keep you company while we're away."

"Magnifique, mes amis. I have the problem you may help me with. The Germans are stuck in the sand a few kilometers from Hassi Messaoud. One of their trucks sunk in the sand and they tried to pull it out with one of their other trucks. Now both trucks are stuck. Would this not be a good test of your Citroën?"

Turning his face away from Lom, Reggie winks at Clive, "What do you think Jonesy?"

"I'm for it," Clive says.

Reggie sets the brandy bottle on Lom's desk. "I think that would make an excellent test captain. How do we find them?"

Lom stands from his chair and goes to a large map on the wall. The cigar bobs up and down in his mouth as he describes the German's location.

"They are about 16 or 17 kilometers southwest of the well."

He points to the location on the map. Running his finger along the map, Lom points out a route for Reggie and Clive to follow.

"Stay on this route. At sixty kilometers you will see the ruins of an old fort. You will find a native man waiting there to take you to the Germans. He is a grey-bearded man we call Sami Akesbi. If he should not be there when you arrive, you will please wait for him. He is to be there in the afternoon of each day until you arrive."

"Were you so sure we would take the job?" Reggie asks.

Lom returns to his chair. "If not you, I would ask Miss Fairthorpe. She and the professor Nast are old friends I think. She is one to make things happen. I fear the Germans will use any means to become unstuck. I do not wish them to harm the natives or the livestock. You are the best solution to avoid troubles. The roads are quite good; your caterpillar should make your travels to the Germans by this afternoon. Bon Voyage, mes amis."

Out in the lot behind the police station Reggie starts the Citroën's engine. Clive climbs in the passenger seat. "I say old scout, that was rather … oh what is the bloody word?"

"Is serendipity what you're looking for?" Reggie asks. "I wonder. I think Lom is very clever. Well there's not much use in mucking about, let's get going."

The Citroën jounces on the hard-packed, but uneven road, kicking up clouds of dust and gravel. Making good time, by early afternoon they stop by the old fort's crumbling stone walls. Stretching as they climb from the Citroën, the men go to the shade provided by what remains of a crumbling stone wall.

Clive shakes his pocket watch then holds it up to his ear. "I say squire, what time do you have? I think the old relic's got sand in it."

Reggie glances at his wristwatch. "I have two forty-five. Let's make some tea. There's no telling how long we'll have to wait."

BOBO'S RAID

Reggie sips from his mug of tea. Leaning on a fender of the Citroën he looks out at the endless rolling dunes.

"Penny for your thoughts, old wise one."

Reggie grins at Clive and nods toward the dunes. "I was thinking of what it must have been like for the poor blokes that had to serve here. We're still in the winter; it must have been hell on earth here in the summer. Every one of these ruins we pass has rows of grave markers."

Reggie raises binoculars to his eyes. Through the lenses he sees the image of a man in robes in the distance. Heat shimmering up from the sands causes an eerie illusion of the man: the Berber seems to float toward him.

Handing the binoculars to Clive, Reggie says, "This must be our guide."

Still some distance away, the man hails them holding his walking stick above his head.

When close, they see a typical Berber, a white turban covering his nut brown head. He is of medium build with the gray beard Lom described. The man wears a long, brown, hooded woolen garment called a jellaba over several other layers of clothing.

Clive offers the man tea. The Berber sniffs, then sips the tea. Reggie offers dates, that the man squeezes over the tea.

"You are Sami?" Reggie asks.

"Oui, Sami," the Berber touches his chest.

"Do you speak English?"

"Non, peu Français."

"What's he say Reggie?" Clive asks.

"I believe he says he speaks a little French," Reggie replies.

Using his hands, as well as his voice, Reggie asks, "Can you take us to the Germans?"

"Oui," the Berber nods.

Sitting in the passenger seat of the Citroën, the Berber points toward the east. With a sweeping motion of his hand, the native looks at Reggie and says, "Allez."

Moving off the road they head over the dunes. The Berber taps Reggie on his knee with the walking stick when he wants a change of direction. Reggie finds driving on constantly shifting sand requires a good bit of concentration. Some areas are deep sand, particularly the lee side of a tall dune. Cresting a dune at times is harrowing. The slope up the dune may be gentle, then at the crest the dune just falls away almost vertically.

Concentrating on the sands when the Berber next taps his knee, Reggie responds with some annoyance. "Just point with your hand, you silly old bugger." Reggie rubs his knee, then bats the Berber's walking stick away.

Crawling along, 4 kilometers takes almost an hour. Coming to the top of a series of dunes, the Berber pounds his stick on the floor between his legs.

"Arrêter, halt, stop."

Reggie stops the Citroën before cresting the dune, but not before the Berber has the door open and is on his way out.

"Mind the track," Clive yells. By the time Clive climbs around the seat to the door, the Berber is moving fast on his way back down the dune.

BOBO'S RAID

"I say, the old boy must be in a hurry to get back to his camels."

Reggie, getting out of the Citroën, walks to the top of the dune. Looking down the gentle slope he sees the two German trucks up to their rear axles in the sand. Turning back to the Citroën he motions to Clive to get in the truck.

"Our friend Sami doesn't seem to want the Jerrys to know he brought us here. Let's go see if we can get them out of the sand. They look stuck good and proper."

At the bottom of the dunes is an area of flat ground. The German campsite is surrounded on three sides by other dunes. A dry river bed snakes through the valleys of the dunes giving access to the campsite. Both of the German trucks are in the middle of the bowl in the deepest sand. The third truck is parked on harder earth by the old river bed. There are six small tents and two larger ones set up near the river bed.

Reggie drives down the slope approaching one of the large tents. A man in a desert brown uniform, his peaked cap pulled low over his eyes, comes out of the tent aiming a rifle at the Citroën. "Halt!" he yells. More men swarm out of the tent. One of the men goes to the rifleman and pushes the gun's muzzle toward the ground.

Stopping the Citroën, Reggie watches the Germans for a moment before speaking quietly to Clive. "Stay in the truck and cover me. If they mean to start trouble shoot the man with the rifle first."

Clive pulls his Webley pistol. "They don't seem the friendly sort old duck. Don't worry; the bloke won't get off a shot."

Moving around the Citroën, Reggie asks who is in charge.

Taking his hand from the rifle's muzzle, the officer steps forward. "I am Major Schulz. You must be the men sent to get our trucks free."

Reggie walks to the officer with his arm extended. "Yes sir, we are. I'm Reggie Bobrowski and my friend in the truck is Clive Parry-Jones."

Major Schulz shakes Reggie's hand, and nods toward the Citroën. "You may tell your friend that it will not be necessary to use his weapon."

"We didn't know what to expect, Major. I'll get my friend and we'll have a look at your trucks."

Reggie motions Clive to join them. "Jonesy, this is Major Schulz. Let's have a look at the trucks."

Major Schulz asks Reggie how he found the German position. Reggie, thinking fast, says, "We were given good instructions and our map shows the dry riverbed. You are just where we expected to find you."

Clive walks ahead to the lead truck, looking under it to see how deep it is in the sand. At the back of the truck he unties a canvas strap to look inside. The big German rifleman appears behind Clive. Using the butt of his rifle, he knocks him to the ground. Standing over Clive with the rifle butt raised, he shouts, "Verboten! No touch."

Chapter 20

Reggie sees Clive hit the sand and rushes over with Major Schulz on his heels.

"Halt Olaf!" the major yells. Olaf slowly lowers his rifle. He and the Major trade some nasty sounding remarks in guttural German.

Reggie, helping Clive up, asks, "What happened, Jonesy?"

"I'm afraid I was rather clumsy Reg. The rear springs sag like the truck still has a heavy load. I wanted to see if the truck is still loaded. I should have asked if I could look inside. Bloody stupid really."

Major Schulz dismisses his soldier and turns to Reggie and Clive. "Is your man all right, Bobrowski? Olaf is somewhat overprotective, I'm afraid."

"Sorry Major," Clive says. "I wasn't thinking. Your truck looks to still have a heavy load in the bed. I was going to have a look. The trucks will have to be as light as you can make them for us to get you out."

"Yes of course," Schulz replies. "We are carrying sensitive materials. I will have both trucks unloaded into the tents. Perhaps you gentlemen will join me in the mess tent for some refreshment while the trucks are unloaded. Please follow me."

Entering the tent, Schulz orders men sitting at tables to unload the trucks. The big German with the rifle grunts an oath and files out of the tent with the other men following. Schulz waves Reggie and Clive to chairs and brings three beers from behind a counter to the table. Putting the beers on the table, Schulz removes his cap to wipe sweat from his forehead.

"Olaf, the man with the rifle, is a party member who would like to think he is in charge here. He is a very serious fellow. It would be best for both of you to give him a wide berth."

Two men burst into the tent: an older man, his face almost beet red, and a young man, both wearing lab coats.

"Major! Oh, excuse me, I see you have guests."

"Professor Nast, this is Reggie Bobrowski and Clive Parry-Jones. These are the men with the Citroën who have come to help us get the trucks out. Herr Bobrowski, Herr Parry-Jones, this is Professor Nast and his assistant Eric Braun. Will you have a beer with us?"

Nast hesitates then walks to the table. "Pleased to meet you gentlemen. Yes, yes, thank you Major, we would like to join you. Eric, get us a drink will you? I was curious as to why the men were bringing the... ah equipment into our tent."

"We need to lighten the trucks, Professor, to make it possible for our friends to pull them out of the sand. Your tent will have to do for the moment."

"Yes I see, Major. I do wish you could do something about Olaf. I find the man insufferable."

"I'm afraid he will be our cross to bear until we are done here professor."

The professor takes the beer from his assistant, then looks at Reggie with an absent stare. "Bobrowski, Bobrowski, Count Bobrowski, was your father Count Bobrowski? A good mind, wasted in a racing car crash as I recall. I knew him at university. He was interested in ancient Roman ideology."

"Yes, Count Bobrowski was my father, however I never thought of his life as being wasted."

"Mien Gott," the professor exclaims. "I apologize. I have no social skill. I liked your father. I did not mean to be rude. But you, too, are the racing driver are you not?"

"Yes, it is a passion I like to think I inherited from my father. Few things in life can make your senses so keen, or make one feel so alive."

"Yes, yes, you are your father's child. Well I must say this is a great pleasure. You look a great deal like your father. I shudder to think of how many years ago we would talk together of ancient history. How do you come to be here? Ach, I know! Following in your father's foot steps. You must be on a grand adventure. Will your adventure allow time for the Tripoli Grand Prix?"

"I do plan a visit to the Grand Prix, but I'm actually here with my friend Clive to test our Citroën. We've modified a Citroën Kégresse truck to tackle the harshest terrains for military transport. We're also interested in the feasibility of extending the railroad system here.

"I didn't know you were a friend of my father's. Perhaps we could have dinner sometime soon and trade stories. I would very much like to hear about your work here also. I've read some of your papers on geology, but you are also an archaeologist?"

The professor looks up from polishing his old fashioned pince-nez glasses. "I am a member of a new society forming in Germany. We are committed to proving the pre-eminence of German peoples in the formation of civilization. As part of this group we are following all the great early civilizations to collect artifacts that will prove our participation in the formation of certain dynasties."

Reggie glances over at Clive who looks back with a bemused wide-eyed stare. "That must be quite a job, professor."

The professor gives Reggie a sly wink. "Oh yes indeed. We are gathering quite a collection."

Major Schulz watches the men converse and adds, "Yes this is special work. Quite important work. The professor is a very skilled archaeologist."

A shaft of sunlight stabs the tent's interior as Olaf pushes back the entrance flap. He confers with the Major, then turns on his heel to exit the tent.

The Major toggles the wire closure on the stopper of his beer bottle. "We have the trucks unloaded gentlemen. Shall we go?"

Blinking in the bright sunshine the men gather around the German trucks. Major Schulz follows Clive and Reggie around the stranded trucks. "How do you want to start, Herr Bobrowski?"

Reggie, pulling on his ear lobe in thought, looks back at the Citroën. "We'll push your trucks out Major. We'll make up some wood beams to fit over the front of the Citroën and mate up to the back of your trucks. Pushing with the Citroën will take weight off the back of your truck and add tractive weight to the Citroën.

"Have your men place some planks under the rear wheels and tell your driver to steer straight, do not turn until we are out of the deep sand. Keep the truck moving and park on the hard ground by the river bed where you have your third truck."

Reggie eases the Citroën behind the lead truck as Clive positions wood beams between the two vehicles to take up the difference in height with the taller German truck's rear end. Reggie drives forward until he has firm contact then adds throttle; the back of the German truck lifts. Clive runs forward to tell the German truck driver to ease on the gas. A cheer goes up from the soldiers watching as the truck's tires find purchase on the wood planks, then drives forward freed from the deep sand.

They repeat the process with the second truck and finally all the German trucks are parked safely by the river bed.

Reggie and Clive remove the wood planks. Getting back in the Citroën, Reggie drives to the center of the valley, across the deepest sand, and, using the caterpillar tracks' steering, he makes sharp turns throwing up plumes of sand. The Citroën snakes over the deep sand, Reggie playfully demonstrating the truck's versatility before driving back to the tents. The soldiers, delighted with the diversion, give a cheer. Schulz invites everyone to the mess tent to celebrate.

Schulz motions Reggie and Clive to sit at a table with Professor Nast and his assistant, Braun. Olaf leads the soldiers to help themselves to beer behind the counter. The major brings cups and a bottle of schnapps on a tray to the table, pours the schnapps, then raises his cup to toast, "Thank you. After all the work we did to try to get the trucks out I would never have believed it would be so easy for you. Your little truck works like magic; here's to you."

Reggie drinks from his cup. "That's good, thank you Major. I'm glad it went so well. Clive and I will be on our way. Professor, I hope we can get together for dinner."

Nast empties his cup before replying, "Eric and I will be coming to Ouargla next week for supplies. I plan to stay at the Europa for several days. After a month in the desert I need to sleep in a real bed and have good food. I would very much like to dine with you and your friend."

"Excellent, Professor," Reggie exclaims. "We will meet you next week at the hotel. Where do you go from here?"

"We have our base in Hassi Messaoud. However it is a place with few amenities I'm afraid."

Reggie pushes back from the table. "We'll report to Captain Lom that you are on your way. He is concerned that you could have some trouble from the Berbers."

Schulz rises from his chair, "What sort of trouble, may I ask?"

"Lom's heard stories that someone is stealing sheep from the Berbers," Reggie replies.

Nast bangs down his cup. "Olaf!"

"That will do Professor," Schulz commands. "I'll take care of Olaf, he is my responsibility." Schulz shakes hands with Clive and Reggie. "Thank you again for your assistance. I hope your stay here will be profitable."

"Thank you Major. We'll be in the region for awhile yet. I'm sure we'll see you again. Come on Jonesy, let's be on our way."

BOBO'S RAID

On the way to the Citroën Reggie whispers to Clive, "We'll drive north, then double back. I want to see what they load in those trucks."

Chapter 21

Driving north several miles to make sure the Germans are not following, the men turn back. They go southeast, keeping well clear of the German encampment, then back toward the camp. Reggie stops just below the ridge of a dune above the camp. With the sun at their backs, Clive and Reggie crawl to the crest. Reggie raises his binoculars to his eyes.

Looking down on the camp he sees men busy loading drilling equipment in one truck. A flash of blinding light strikes his eyes. Reggie instinctively ducks his head and reaches out to push Clive's head to the sand.

Clive squirms backwards out from under Reggie's hand. Brushing sand from his face he sees Reggie motioning him to stay down under the crest of the dune.

"I say, thanks awfully, old brute. What's the trouble?"

"Sorry Jonesy, someone down there is scanning the dunes with binoculars. The sun's reflection off the lenses almost blinded me. I'm going to dig out some sand so my head is below the peak and see if we've been spotted."

Reggie takes a brief look through the binoculars, then a long slow scan. Moving down from the ridge, he hands the binoculars to Clive.

BOBO'S RAID

"Take a look but be careful. The major is scanning the dunes with his binoculars. I think they're loading one of the trucks with mining equipment. See what you think."

Clive has a look, then returns to Reggie's position.

"They've got drilling equipment in one truck and it looks like mining equipment going in the other truck. Maybe the mining equipment is what they use for digging up the artifacts they're looking for. Some of the men are taking down the tents so I think they're going to pull out soon. You think the Major saw us?"

Reggie shakes his head. "No I don't think so. He had to be looking right into the sun. I don't know if he was looking for us or the Berbers. Let's get going before they're mobile. We can get back to Ouargla and make a report to our good friend Claire. The professor will be in town soon and I'd like to spend some time on the radio with Ally. Fay's sure to want to know how you're doing."

Driving back to Ouargla though the fading daylight, the dunes flatten out. As day ends, the desert, barren of any light, gives a grand view of the black sky sprinkled with millions of stars. It is past midnight by the time they are back in their rooms at the Europa Hotel.

Both men are at breakfast by 7am the next day, anxious to make their reports to both Captain Lom and the Prime Minister through S's radio operator. Lom enters the restaurant and looks around the room. A brief grin forms on his face when he spots Clive and Reggie. On the way to their table he snags a coffee cup from another table. Pulling out a chair, Lom seats himself and pours coffee from the pot on the men's table.

"Good morning to you, mes amis. You have the success with our German friends?"

Reggie smiles, toasting Lom with his coffee cup. "Nice to see you, Captain. And yes, we were able to get their trucks going quite easily. They were on their way to Hassi Messaoud when we left them."

"Excellent, they are quiet there and will not make trouble for me. They dig for their artifacts and find water with the bad smells. I think it is the oil they are here for. Is this not so?"

Taken aback, Reggie is a little slow to reply, "I don't know about that Captain. The Professor said they are looking for artifacts that would prove the German people had a hand in the earliest civilizations. That sounds a bit far-fetched to me, but that's all I know about it."

With a shrug of indifference Lom says, "It is of the small importance to me. If they find oil they will not be able to harvest it without the permission of my government. Unless, of course, if they could make it a prize of war. The papers are full of the strutting magpies beating the drums of hate and war. Our Maginot digs the tunnels to protect us from the Boche. It is the folly, do you not think this?"

"I think you have too much on your mind, Captain. Have some breakfast; the world will look brighter on a full stomach."

"You are, of course, correct Reginald. As you English say, there is nothing for it as maniacs reign." Lom raises his cup. "Here is to better days, mes amis."

Between mouthfuls of breakfast Clive describes how they got the German trucks out of the deep sand and the run in with the big Nazi Olaf Fischer. Lom asks for details on the German camp and the big Nazi. Putting his napkin down Lom pushes back from the table to light his cigar. When the dark tobacco glows red, Lom's head tilts back as he exhales a long plume of smoke. "What is your plan for this week?"

"After breakfast we're going to the Citroën and spend some time on the radio with our wives. I learned that Professor Nast was an old friend of my father's. He's coming into Ouargla for supplies this week and we're going to have dinner. I'm looking forward to the professor's stories of university days with my father."

Lom stands up from his chair. "Perhaps dinner later in the week. Adieu, gentlemen."

Clive untucks his napkin and pushes back from the table. "I'll go make the report to Claire's people while you talk with Ally. It'll give you a chance for some privacy. I'll meet you back here for lunch. I'll radio Fay after lunch."

"Thanks Jonesy, see you later."

Reggie spends the next two hours catching up with his wife on the radio set in the Citroën. After they each profess the pains of missing each other, Ally brings Reggie up to date on his business holdings. Reggie writes down the business tasks he needs to take care of and, before he signs off, he asks if the Bugatti team has a car for him to drive at Tripoli. Alexandra answers affirmatively.

Reggie eagerly punches the send button on the radio.

"Ally, I want you to come, I really miss you. I don't know how much longer this business here is going to take. Please come; you can take the train to Rome and fly across to Tripoli from there. You could bring Fay with you. You'll have a travelling companion and… I can't wait to see you sweetheart.

"This is going to be a grand event. After that lottery fiasco, the Italians have promised to make this year the best ever. The weather will be sunny and hot, you'll be out of the English rain and tanning in the sun."

Reggie locks up the Citroën then goes to the restaurant to wait for Clive. Looking over the empty tables he takes a seat realizing how eager he is to see Ally. Daydreaming of driving the new Bugatti at Tripoli, he drinks in the sounds and smells of Grand Prix racing. He looks toward the restaurant's entrance, anxious to relay the good news to Clive. After draining two cups of coffee and no sign of Clive, Reggie orders lunch.

Chapter 22

After lunch Reggie checks Clive's room. Finding no response at the room, he heads toward S's men's radio room. The room is located by a busy market next to a mosque. Men and women are milling about the various stalls that are covered by brightly colored awnings. The air is filled with the noise of voices in Berber and broken French.

Some voices rise to be heard over the din; deals are being made. Everything from goat's heads with their strange eyes staring into the distance to date breads are sold or bartered in the clamor.

Reggie picks his way through the crowd dropping some coins to the more insistent beggars. Breaking free of the market, Reggie passes the tall mosque tower. Looking up at the tower, his eyes follow a black wire running up to the top to an antenna perched atop the tower. Following the same wire down it leads to the top floor of an adjacent building.

Climbing the narrow stairway of the building, Reggie knocks on the door at the head of the stairway. Waiting a moment he raps harder on the heavy door. A steel plate covering a hole bored into the thick door slides open. Terry Mays's face appears, the plate slides shut, iron bolts clank back and the door opens.

"Hello Reggie, welcome to my little warren."

Reggie walks into the room which is not quite the little warren. The room is actually the entire upper floor of the building. Looking the room over, Reggie thinks it is probably five to six hundred square feet of space. Bars placed on the inside of the four large windows and the size of the door bolts tell of the security measures in place.

A second door to the outside has a rope ladder hanging on pegs beside it. On the far side of the room a cot with a chamber pot under it is partially hidden behind a partition. A counter on the back wall has a hot plate hosting a battered coffee pot. On the wall facing the stairway door is a rack with various weapons. Rifles, pistols, gas and fragmenting grenades are placed in quick reach along with several gas masks. The huge old radio sets are against a wall without windows. Reggie looks over the radios with interest.

"Your little warren seems well prepared for a major assault. I'm a bit surprised by the radios though. Your Mr. Smyth claims these are the latest models."

"He ain't my Mr. Smyth. I'm the PM's man remember? As to the weapons, the Berbers could have a major uprising at anytime. The last time some drunken French soldier pissed on the side of a mosque we all feared for our lives. It's a powder keg here that could go off in an instant."

"Sorry Terry, I'm a little worried about Clive. We were supposed to meet for lunch after he gave our report to you or Miss Fairthorpe. He didn't show up for lunch, I can see he's not here. Do you know where he is?"

"He left when Claire and Clarkson went out a few hours ago. Maybe they had lunch together. Claire sent me out before Clive got here to run some errands for her. I think she wanted to get rid of me while he was here. I don't see a transcript of his report and I don't know that Clarkson was sober enough to send one anyway."

Reggie glances around the room again before turning back to Mays. "Well okay, I guess I'll go back to the hotel and see if Jonesy has shown up. By the way, you can tell the PM that Captain Lom thinks the Jerrys have found oil around Hassi Messaoud."

"I'll send that off now. Don't worry Count; your man'll be okay. If Clarkson can stumble around this place unmolested, it's gotta' be pretty safe for now."

Chapter 23

Ouargla sprawls for many miles over the landscape in every direction. Reggie skirts the market, wandering the dusty narrow streets in an effort to find Clive. After an hour of looking into the small shops and food stalls he realizes the futility of his search.

Heading back to the hotel Reggie thinks briefly of going to Lom's. His mind swirls with strange images. Coming to an intersection a horn blares making him jump back to get clear of a truck piled high with wine barrels. Stopped in his tracks he thinks, "What in the hell am I doing? Clive's a grown man, he doesn't need me looking after him." But he can't quite shake his feeling of unease. His mood lifts when, at the top of the stairway at the hotel, he sees Clive walking toward him down the hallway.

"Jonesy, I've been looking for you."

"I'm just on my way out, old man."

"Aren't you having dinner with the professor and me tonight?"

Clive continues past. "Sorry can't be done. I need a night on my own, old drone."

"I've got good news, Clive. I've invited the wives to come to Tripoli for the Grand Prix."

"For God's sake Reg, don't you think you should have asked me first?"

"I thought you'd be over the moon. Let's have a beer and talk it over."

Talking over his shoulder without making eye contact Clive says, "Tomorrow. I want to take in the city tonight."

"What's the hurry? You can see the city any time."

"Let it go Reggie, we're not joined at the hip you know. I'll see you in the morning."

Without a pause Clive walks down the stairs. "I wonder what's eating him?" Reggie mutters. "Not joined at the hip?"

Reggie studies his face in the shaving mirror, his unease over Clive's missing their lunch seems silly now. The blade of the straight razor his father gave him gleams in the mirror's light and glides smoothly over his face. The familiar mother of pearl handle feels good in his hand; his brown eyes smile back at him. Dinner with Nast will be interesting, but he can't stop thinking about being with Ally in Tripoli.

With a spring in his step, Reggie trots down the stairs to the restaurant. Captain Lom is at a table with three other men but raises his glass as Reggie enters. Professor Nast stands by his table to motion Reggie over. They shake hands. Nast, pouring wine, says, "Have a seat Count."

"Please call me Reggie, Professor."

"Oh, but I quite like your title. Dinner, with a Count who is the son of an old friend, in the middle of the world's largest desert, seems almost impossible. I have been dreaming of a good meal for a long time. I think this is the best European-type restaurant south of Algiers.

"I'm afraid roaming the desert tasting the sand is not my calling. But enough of my plight, my boy." The professor looks up from his wine glass with a mischievous grin. "How goes your quest for the Mali gold?"

Reggie, almost spilling his wine, sits the glass down and laughs. "Mali gold is the last thing on my mind Professor. The Citroën and a railroad survey are the reasons I'm here. That, and having a good excuse for being out of the English winter."

"Ah, but the desert winds say that you are digging the sands, so what other than gold are you after?"

"Clive and I dug a water well for a Berber family. We found the man of the place neck-deep in sand with his two sons about to go under with him. We did strike water right where the man was digging."

Nast packs his black wood pipe with tobacco from a scuffed leather pouch. "So it is a noble cause that has you digging, not the hunt for treasure."

"That's the only digging I've done. Have you had any luck with your digging?"

"Touché." Nast laughs. "I think we both roam the desert for our own purposes, but enough of rumors. I have read that you are successful with your racing in England. What car do you have for the race in Tripoli?"

Reggie relaxes in his chair. "I'll be racing a Bugatti."

Nast shakes his head. "No I think not. My information is that Bugatti will not come to Tripoli. Our Mercedes and Auto Union cars are too strong now. Only Alfa and Maserati will oppose our cars."

"You seem well informed Professor. When did you learn of this?"

BOBO'S RAID

"I have your father to thank for my interest in auto racing. When we were in college, he would hound the bookstores to stock the latest racing papers. He was a great admirer of Mercedes, as am I. My good friend, Adolf Huhnlein, is the Director of Motorsports. That, my boy, is my little joke. The Korpfüher has few friends in Motorsports. However, he has directed his office to keep me informed of all German Motorsports.

"Monsieur Bugatti's cars are no longer competitive; his ideas are outdated. It may be that his company no longer has the funds to compete. Our German cars are quite advanced. I believe it will be our cars racing against each other for the wins."

Reggie taps a cigarette on the back of his silver case. "I've read all the trades to see the Mercedes and Auto Union designs. I want to see them for myself and I want to be at Tripoli. I already made plans to be there with my wife and friends. I haven't driven on the race course there. From what I read it's bloody fast and over eight miles long. I think if I start phoning soon I can line up a Maser to drive. It would probably be faster than the Bugatti anyway."

"I envy your youth Count, off racing without a care. I will not be racing, but I will enjoy watching our Grand Prix teams race to glory. We call them the Silver Arrows in my homeland. I hope we will not see more of that abominable cheating they performed in '33."

"I don't know Professor, I'm not sure it was as bad as some people reported. When Mussolini started the Italian lottery and made the grand prize contingent on the Grand Prix winner someone should have given the rules more thought. I know Nuvolari and Varzi entered into an agreement with four other drivers to divide the lottery money between them, and Varzi won the coin toss to be the winner.

"I understand the agreement was written up by an Italian lawyer and was quite legal. So Varzi won, Nuvolari ran out of petrol and had to get his crew to put a splash in his car to finish a close second. It did look suspect I agree. They also partied long into the night with the most expensive champagne money could buy. That certainly added to the legend. The big problem with the lottery was declaring the ticket holder a winner weeks before the race.

"That way the man with the winning ticket could try to buy the drivers. Then if his driver won he would win even more lira. They changed the rules now, so that the lottery ticket is drawn only minutes before the race.

Professor Nast leans back in his chair as the waiter places the first course of the meal in front of him. "I must say that I am looking forward to the first Grand Prix of the season. It is also a good excuse to sleep in a good hotel and not the retched tent in the sand. I will be happy to be home before the summer heat hits here. We have one more dig in Tamanrasset to complete before leaving for Germany."

Reggie pats his mouth with his napkin. "When do you leave for Tamanrasset?"

"As soon as I return from Libya. Major Schulz was quite unhappy to have me leave until I invited him to join me for the Grand Prix. Our supply plane will take us there. Why don't you and your friend join us?"

"That is most kind of you. We will be delighted to make the trip with you. I may be able to return the favor. We're headed toward Tamanrasset also, to map a railroad route. You could radio us if you need assistance."

Nast's brow wrinkles, he clears his throat before speaking. "I had no idea you had any interest in Tamanrasset. I do not want to seem rude but I do not think the major would like the idea of you traveling with us."

"You needn't worry, Professor, we couldn't keep up with you. I have to survey the best route for train tracks. That means I must find not only the shortest route, but the way with fewest obstacles. We won't stay in Tamanrasset. That will be the end of our business here and we can be home for the first races at Brooklands. I mentioned the radio contact in case your trucks were to get stuck again."

"That is kind of you Count, I will talk with Schulz. We can discuss the matter on the way to Tripoli. This is an excellent wine, but this is the third bottle of it today. Let's order some good champagne. I'll tell you some stories of your father and me when we were in university."

Nast tells Reggie about wild trips in the Count's huge Rolls Royce: how they would barrel down narrow country lanes to get to a race, then when the race was over the Count would jump back into the Rolls to get them back to school before Monday.

"I could not believe the Rolls could be driven like that. We had a few close calls. The Count went to sleep one night and we both awoke to a curious cow's wet nose squeaking against the car's window. I can tell you waking to see that nose and the huge eyes staring in gave us quite a start. We were in the middle of a pasture having crashed through an old wood fence. We had a devil of a time getting the car out. Your father insisted that we find the owner of the farm so we could repair the fence before we were on our way again. I am not used to this champagne, the room's beginning to spin."

Nast stands from his chair holding on to the chair back for support.

"Let me help you to your room Professor."

Reggie supports Nast, guiding him from the restaurant to his room upstairs. Nast misses a step and Reggie grabs the professor around the waist to keep him from falling.

At the professor's door Reggie stays to be sure Nast can get into his room. "Goodnight Professor, I'll see you in the morning."

Nast, swaying to the beat of the wine, fumbles with his room key trying to find the lock to open his door. Reggie takes the key and opens the door. Nast, holding on to the door jamb, looks at Reggie as if surprised to see him. "Oh g'night Count Reg-nald, was nice. Schulz'll be watching, don't you worry. We're not after what you think we are. Ach, said too much now, better go to bed."

Chapter 24

Reggie wakes well after sunup. After a shower and shave, he knocks on the door to Clive's room. With no response after knocking again, he heads downstairs to the restaurant. Professor Nast sits at a table adorned with a coffee urn, aspirin bottle, and a glass of tomato juice.

"May I join you Professor?"

The little man looks up with tired bloodshot eyes, then chuckles. "You may if you promise not to shout anymore. I feel the fool Count. My first day back in civilization and I drink too much. I hope I did not embarrass you, my boy. I do not remember much after the second bottle of champagne."

"Not to worry sir. You were the perfect gentleman as always."

"You are too kind Count. I miss the winter of home. I enjoy the snow. Skiing in the mountains and skating on the frozen lakes are two of my favorite things. You must concentrate on both endeavors. The crisp clean cold air clears the mind of all other problems. I'm afraid the vast emptiness of the desert does not agree with me."

Nast sits up in his chair looking over Reggie's shoulder. "I believe we have a guest."

"Bobrowski, I need a word." Reggie turns at the female's voice to see Claire Fairthorpe glaring down at him.

"Do you have something to say that can't be said here?"

Nast clears his throat. "Please be mindful of my fragile head."

"Sorry professor." Reggie notes the professor's pinched face. "Excuse us please."

Reggie stands from his chair and follows Claire out of the restaurant and through the lobby to outside the front entrance. Claire turns to Reggie with a hard look, her hands on her hips.

"You may go off on your adolescent lark, but you will leave Parry-Jones here to continue the work that needs to be done. Do you understand me?"

"No, Miss Fairthorpe, I don't. Clive is coming with me to Tripoli. His wife will be anxious the see him. I have cleared this with the PM."

She thrusts her face up to his, biting off her words. "Clive does not want to go with you. You may go, you are of little help or importance to me. I do not want you to try to contact Clive. Just be on your way, you two are not joined at the hip."

"Ah, I see, joined at the hip. You think you have collected another slave to your service. I'll do everything in my power to pull Clive from your grip. You can tell him, if you dare, that he can not be any kind of man if he abandons his wife and friends to your seduction. I know Jonesy. He's a good man, he'll soon see through of your… ah, dubious charms."

Reggie jerks his arm up in time to block Claire's fist. She pulls back and kicks out at him. Reggie turns to his side in time to deflect her foot that grazes his thigh. Her face blotches red with fury as she screams, "You are a fool. The clown Bobo. I can have you eliminated at the snap of my fingers."

"I'll be sure to pass that along to the PM." Reggie turns his back to her almost expecting to feel her claws tear his flesh. People in the hotel lobby stare at him as he goes back to the restaurant.

Professor Nast puts down a tall glass, red clumps of juice with black speckles run back down the inside of the glass. His face pulled to a grimace, the professor slowly shakes his head. Wiping his mouth on a napkin, he gestures for Reggie to sit.

"This terrible concoction the waiter came up with may have saved my life. Please sit with me; I may require resuscitation."

Reggie chuckles, gently kneads the old man's shoulder, and sits down.

"You're getting some color back in your face Professor. You may yet live."

"As the saying goes, no fool like an old fool. Be that as it may, I must tell you I am concerned for you, my boy. Claire Fairthorpe is not a woman to trifle with. She can be as deadly as her father was. I knew the man, and I can tell you that her father was a double agent in the South African wars. My country hanged him for his treachery. She, I fear, is the proverbial apple fallen close to the tree. This is a dangerous place. Out in the desert there is no law. Please be careful.

"You should also be wary of Olaf. He is a Nazi thug. I believe he and Miss Fairthorpe are…shall we say intimate. She uses men for purposes that suit her. This Olaf, however, could be her undoing; he is as unscrupulous as she. I am positive it was Olaf that killed a Berber girl. She was just a poor young girl who did nothing but spurn Olaf's advances. Schulz says there is not enough proof that Olaf did it.

"You are much like your father. You remind me of my youth. We were young and foolish and most probably should not have survived our youth. I do not wish any harm to come to you my boy. I can not say more, and I will not be able to speak candidly when Major Schulz is with us. I need breakfast now, something to absorb the remaining alcohol in my system."

Leaving Nast, Reggie goes back to his room to formulate a plan to find Clive. He is reluctant to bring Lom into the picture for fear of having his real mission revealed. Clive's almost certain infidelity is a worry. Reggie and his wife have been friends with Clive and Fay for many years. Reggie does not want word to spread that Clive is Claire Fairthorpe's latest conquest.

Reggie spends the morning going to places in the city he and Clive have frequented, leaving messages for Clive to contact him. He returns to the hotel feeling frustrated. The day grinds on before he decides to use the time to try to find a Maserati to drive in Tripoli.

Arranging to hire a car for the race takes hours due to the time it takes to place a phone call and the negotiations required. Finally, through a contact in England, Reggie is satisfied that he will have a decent car to compete in the race. With his stomach growling, he heads to the restaurant.

Captain Lom enters the restaurant, notes Reggie seated alone, and after fetching a bottle of wine and two glasses from the bar, sits down.

BOBO'S RAID

Pouring the wine Lom asks, "How are you mon ami? I have not seen your friend Jonesy with you."

Reggie raises his glass in salute. "He's on the quest to find the Berber way of life. We have a few days before we're off to Tripoli, so he's soaking up the local culture."

"The little birds tell me the terrible Claire wants her claws in you. Did you not have the disagreement?"

"Yes, well, a disagreement. She is a hard woman to deal with. She thinks helping the Berber family will lead to trouble. I don't see how it could. I have been trying to find her to apologize. Do you know where she lives?"

"I know of several places she stays. I know also she is not what she wishes to me to think. What I do not know is who she works for. We should have dinner first, then you can come to my office and I will show you on the city map where she stays."

After dinner the two men walk to Lom's office. The captain offers one of his black cigars to Reggie who shakes his head to decline. Lom lights his, and opens a window in his office to let the warm dry desert air swirl his heavy cigar smoke like ocean waves. With the cigar held between his fingers, Lom points to the city map on the wall.

"She has rooms on the third floor in this place on the Rue Messaoud." Lom taps the map moving to the west. "Here is where she keeps her car." The ash from his cigar falls to the floor as he taps the map again. Kicking the ash away Lom says, "The British keep this place by the bazaar. It has a radio and a cache of weapons." Lom turns to Reggie with a wink. "I am not supposed to know of the weapons, I think."

"Thank you Captain, I think I'll check her room to see if she's there. I'll see you later."

The building on Rue Messaoud is the same as many of the homes in the city. It is a square structure with a flat, high-walled roof that opens to the elements. The whitewashed walls are stained at street level with the dust and dirt blown by the wind and traffic. Reggie climbs the stairs to the third floor to knock on the weathered dark wood door.

Reggie knocks again and listens for any movement from inside. Growing impatient he pounds on the door then tries the doorknob. The doorknob turns and Reggie opens the door to find an empty room. "Is anyone here?" he calls out.

Walking through the rooms, he sees dishes in a kitchen sink, an unmade bed in the bedroom. Opening the armoire, there are no clothes hanging and nothing in the drawers. The bathroom is empty; no toiletries are in the open cabinet. A brown-colored medicine bottle, along with a half dozen pills, is lying in a sink.

"Looks as though she left in a hurry," Reggie mutters.

Lom said he would find Fairthorpe's car two blocks down an alley from the room on the Rue Messaoud. The lot is empty. On his way back to the hotel, Reggie decides to stop by Claire's radio room office.

The market place is quiet. The vender's stalls are closed or taken down, leaving dark holes in the night. There is no answer to his knocking on the door to the radio room.

Reggie, hands in his pockets, trudges back to the hotel. The man behind the hotel desk motions to him, waving a message paper. The message is from Lom; one of Lom's policemen found Clive unconscious in an alley.

Chapter 25

Reggie turns on his heel and rushes to the police station. Skirting around the officer manning the front desk, he goes directly into Lom's office. Lom is poised with his feet up on his desk, a cigar clamped in his mouth. Even with the window open, the smoke from the cigar lowers the ceiling to just above Reggie's head.

"Where's Clive?"

Lom's chair creaks as he sits up, then rises. "I have him in the back; I brought the post's doctor to look at him."

"You have him in a cell? What did he do?"

Lom leads the way to the jail cells. "I have him there because he has the bad stomach." The heavy steel door creates an unearthly screech on its dry hinges. The entrance reveals rows of flat steel bars riveted together to form four cells. Pinching his nose he turns to Reggie. "My cigars can not mask your friend's offenses to the nose."

Clive lies prone on a bare wood framed bed dressed only in his underclothes. Beads of sweat roll off his ashen face. The doctor wipes Clive's sweat away with a cloth and rises from his seat. Picking up his bag, he points to Clive, then speaks to Lom in rapid French. The doctor bats away the cigar smoke, then whisks the cigar from Lom's mouth and crushes it under his foot.

BOBO'S RAID

Reggie sits on the stool by Clive's bed. Reaching out, Reggie puts his hand on Clive's arm. The skin on his arm is warm and wet. The networks of blood vessels are visible against the pale skin.

The doctor leans down giving Reggie the cloth he used, and squeezes Reggie's shoulder reassuringly.

"Es okay," the doctor says, nodding his head up and down before turning to leave.

Looking down with some sadness on the crushed remains of his cigar Lom explains the doctor's comments to Reggie. "My once friend, the doctor, believes your man was poisoned with a sedative. Monsieur Jones is out of the danger. Whatever was in his stomach is in that bucket that I hope you will empty to the outside."

"That's a good idea, Captain. If you'll open the back door I'll get rid of it."

Returning to Clive's cell ,Reggie sits down as the captain clamps another cigar in his mouth before heading back to his office. Some color begins to return to Clive's face. His eyelids flutter, then weakly open. Clive stares at the ceiling of the cell for a few minutes trying to collect himself, before he notices Reggie. "Oh god, I'm so sorry Reg."

Reggie squeezes Clive's arm. "Not to worry, old sport. I'll go get you some clean clothes from the hotel and we'll get you out of here."

Clive turns his head away and closes his eyes.

Clive is shivering in a cold sweat when Reggie returns from the hotel. Reggie struggles to get Clive's upper body raised enough to get a shirt on him.

"Jonesy, you're gonna have to help me here. Come on, get up. Let's have your pants on and go to the hotel.

You can take a warm bath in the tub and get cleaned up. Come on, up with you, old sport."

Clive rallies enough to swing his legs out of the bunk, stand unsteadily, and pull up his pants. "I, I, don't know what came over me."

"Not now, wait till you feel better. Take a bath, we'll have something to eat. We can talk then."

Reggie puts his arm around Clive's waist to support him as they head to the hotel.

The bathroom window lets in the night's cool desert air. Clive's head is barely visible through the clouds of steam rising from the tub.

Reggie opens the bathroom door just enough to put his head in. "I've got hot tea with biscuits and honey as soon as you drag your backside out of the bath. The doctor said you'd been drugged. I'd like to hear all about your adventures with Ouargla nightlife."

Clive emerges from the bathroom pulling closed a long maroon robe. He has a white towel wound around his neck under the robe. Crossing the room he sits down on a chair by a small table holding the tea and biscuits. Reggie pours tea in a cup for Clive, then sits back in his chair waiting for Clive to speak.

Clive picks up the cup ignoring the biscuits and avoiding Reggie's eyes.

"So what happened Jonesy? You're not the first guy to get drugged and rolled. Lom says he's closed a dozen bars that robbed the soldiers in this town. It's nothing to be ashamed of old man."

Clive sips his tea looking down into the cup.

"Reg, I'd like to tell you that's what happened, but I don't want to lie."

Reggie watches Clive's forlorn face stare into the teacup.

"Ah, so I take it a woman was involved. Is that it?"

Clive starts, he looks at Reggie with surprise in his eyes, then quickly looks away.

"Come on, old man, we're men of the world. Did you meet her after you went to see the Fairthorpe woman?" Reggie stops talking and looks at Clive who is almost curling in on himself. "Oh my God! It wasn't Claire Fairthorpe was it?"

Clive leaps from his chair, and darts to the bathroom with his hand clamped over his mouth. A few minutes later he exits the bathroom wiping his mouth with a towel. Returning to the chair, his face devoid of color, Clive sits down, blowing out a long sigh.

"I can't believe I did it. There was just something about her that really excited me. We went to dinner after I gave her our report and…I don't know, she just mesmerized me. She took me to her house after dinner and we…"

"Look, Jonesy old man you don't have to spell it out for me. I get the picture. What you may not yet realize is Claire Fairthorpe does that sort of thing as part of her job. She likes having control. You don't have to be embarrassed. I'll get on to the PM. I can't understand how she thought she would get away with this unless she thought she killed you.

"You don't get it at all, old fellow. She positively hates you; it kills her that she can't bend you to her will. I'm thinking now that she seduced me just to get back at you. The woman wants to ruin both of us, but I don't think she wanted to kill me. She thinks we found that Mali gold. I told her we didn't but she won't believe me. She said Mr. S is convinced that the only reason we came here was to get our hands on the gold. He told her that he sent the tax boys to search the Reading house, and that they found some ancient coins."

Reggie puts down his teacup and pushes it away. "Of course they found old coins. You know my father collected old coins; you were with me when I bought that old odd-looking gold coin in Jerusalem. Ally told me on the radio that Inland Revenue men came to the house.

"Those coins are registered with our insurance company and the taxes have been paid on them. The men made an inventory of the collection and left. I think that idiot S is just trying to stir something up."

Clive continues to stare into his teacup. "You can't tell the PM Reg. If you do, Claire will tell Fay. I've never cheated on Fay. I don't know what to do. I feel like such a cur. Should I call her Reg?"

Reggie can see the anguish in his friends face. "Why don't you think on it a while old friend. You need to get some sleep. We'll talk about it more in the morning after you've had something to eat."

Chapter 26

Reggie wakes to a banging noise on his door. Rubbing his eyes, he pushes back the bedcovers and climbs out of the bed. The door rattles in the frame from more pounding. "All right I'm coming, stop beating on the door."

Terry Mays bursts past as Reggie opens the door. Mays turns to Reggie breathlessly, "I just got off the radio with the PM's man. Mr. S was arrested for embezzling government funds and selling arms to Turkey."

"Sit down Mays and catch your breath; I'll get some water."

Pouring water into two glasses, Reggie gives a glass to Mays and takes a long drink from his own glass.

"Okay, start from the beginning, will you?"

Mays gulps water from the glass, then looks at Reggie, his eyes wide. "I haven't heard anything from Claire in days, so I went to the radio room this morning. As soon as I put in my call sign the PM's operator gave me an ear-full." Putting the glass down his hand shakes, sloshing water out of the glass.

"Anyway, Smyth implicated Fairthorpe and Clarkson along with several other people under interrogation. The prison guards found our old friend

Smyth dead in his cell this morning. He had some kind of death pill, maybe one of those cyanide jobs.

"The PM wants us to detain Fairthorpe and Clarkson. I think they've been tipped off. The radio room's a mess, and the guns are gone. I went to Claire's house and it's empty; Clarkson's place is too."

Reggie lifts a pillow on his bed to get his pistol. Pulling on clothes and a jacket, he puts the gun in an inside pocket. "I don't suppose you know where Fairthorpe and Clarkson are headed, do you?"

Mays rises from his seat. "I haven't the foggiest. They could have gone in any direction."

Reggie opens the door. "Let's start at the radio room. Did you check the message pad for any writing impressions?"

"I didn't think about that," Mays replies as they go down the hallway. "I thought I should come get you and we'd think of something. My car's out front, but I don't have a gun."

"We need to check the radio room first. I have more weapons in the Citroën if we need them. But there isn't any reason to rush about needlessly. I would think they are going to go north and there's only one road for them to travel. The problem is we have no authority to stop them and no way to get ahead of them.

Reggie pulls open the door. "I'll radio the PM when we get to the radio room. You can look for anything that might put us on their trail. If we do find Claire and Clarkson, we'll have to kidnap them to get them back to England. I'll ask the PM straight up if that's what he wants. If he says yes, then he'll have to send us a plane or have someone cover the road north."

Chapter 27

In a small pool of light from a low-watt bulb, Claire Fairthorpe struggles with a five-gallon can of gasoline. The dim light hanging from the storage hut outlines two cars pulled close together. The gas filler on her car is higher than she can knee up the heavy can. Grunting, she gets the nozzle in the filler neck and lifts the can from her knee.

"When you get your car filled, Clarkson, take Olaf back to his truck. I'll meet you in Tripoli. Give me the code book. I'll get a message to our German friends so we can meet with them when they see the professor."

Clarkson spins the lid off a jerry can. "I don't have the codes. If you don't have it, the book's still in the radio room."

Claire throws her empty can to the ground. "You idiot, go back and get the code book. We need it to sign in. We'll have to meet in Touggourt, you know the place."

Olaf grabs Claire's arm. "What about the gold? You know where it is, don't you? I want my share."

Claire pulls her arm away. "This is not the time to go into that. We have to get to Tripoli, and you need to get back to your expedition. After we receive our orders from your masters we'll come back here.

"Bobrowski is going to fly with the professor to Tripoli and then back to Ouargla after the race. We can grab him then and make him tell us where the gold is."

Clarkson pulls his prized model A Ford coupe up to Olaf's truck on the eastern outskirts of Ouargla. Olaf opens the door to get out. He turns to Clarkson, jaw set, his eyes hard. "If you, or Claire, are thinking about keeping the gold to yourselves, I'll find you wherever you are."

"Olaf, I'm not convinced there is any gold. If there is, you'll get what's coming to you. Now be a good lad and go frighten your own lot."

The Ford speeds off in a cloud of dust before Olaf can close the car's door.

Clarkson drives past the marketplace looking for any sign of movement around the radio room. Backing the Ford into an alley two blocks away, he walks to the radio room. Taking the steps two at a time he listens at the door, then opens it slowly to peer into the dark space. After his eyes adjust to the dark and he is satisfied no one is there, he creeps in.

Snapping on the light he sees the room is not as he and Claire left it. Clarkson smiles and mutters to himself. "Ah my friend Mays has tidied up. What a good little pup he is."

Down on his hands and knees, he crawls under the radio table to find the code book in a wooden pocket he cleverly screwed to the bottom of the table. Coming up off the floor under the table, he hears footsteps on the stairs. Clarkson pulls a pistol from his pocket as he sprints to the rear door. He yanks open the door and throws the rope ladder out just as Reggie opens the front door forcing Clarkson to jump. Running to the rear door, Reggie pulls the pistol from his coat. Clarkson lies on the ground, struggling to get up. Seeing Reggie at the door, he raises his pistol and fires four shots. Reggie falls back into the radio room.

Mays runs to Reggie, staying low, away from the rear door opening.

"Are you hit?"

Reggie sits up, his hand going to his right leg. Blood seeps from his pant leg.

"Take a look and see if Clarkson is gone. Be careful, just a peek, don't get shot."

Mays crawls cautiously to the door. Slowly edging to the opening, head low to the floor, he sees Clarkson hobbling off around the building.

Mays hears Reggie speak in a low voice, "Do you see him?"

Turning back to Reggie, Mays stands up. In the modest light of the room he can see blood soaking through Reggie's pant leg. "He's gone around the building. Looks like he may have hurt himself jumping out of here."

Reggie struggles to get up. "Help me up! We may be able to get him yet."

"You're bleeding a lot. You need a doctor."

"I don't think it's too bad Mays. Just give me a hand up."

Mays bends behind Reggie's back putting his arms around the Count to pull him to his feet.

Reggie looks down at the floor to find his pistol. "Grab my pistol and let's get after him."

Mays picks up the gun and hands it to Reggie. He turns to run out of the stairway door. Almost to the door he hears a crash behind him. Reggie is lying face down on the floor, blood running down his cheek.

Chapter 28

Reggie brings his hand up to shade his eyes. Strong light makes his head hurt. A man with a silver disc on his head lifts Reggie's hand away to examine his eyes.

"Other than the leg, he's fine," the French doctor explains to the men in the hospital room.

Captain Lom looks down at Reggie. "I was afraid for the supply of your wonderful brandy. My friend, the doctor, tells me the lump on your head is nothing. Your friend Clive tells me it is fortunate that you are hard in the head."

"If my head did not hurt so I might find some humor in that. What the deuce happened?"

Terry Mays looks on from the other side of the bed. "After Clarkson shot you, we were going after him. You fell and hit your head on the side of the table. Blood was everywhere; I thought you were dead. I went to the captain and he summoned an ambulance to bring you to the hospital."

Reggie yanks the covers off his legs. Looking down he sees his right leg bandaged from upper thigh to below the knee. "Thank god, I just had the horrible thought they'd wacked off my leg. Tripoli is next week, I'll need to get this bandaging off to drive."

"I don't think that's on, old man," Clive says from the foot of the bed. "The doctor says you have some muscle damage, you're lucky to be able to limp your way out of here."

"Double bugger! As soon as I get rid of this headache I'll see what the old leg will stand. Tell me you at least got Clarkson. Mays, did you get him?"

"Sorry, he's in the wind along with Fairthorpe. I reported the radio room thefts to Captain Lom. He issued a warrant for Clarkson's arrest for assault and robbery. I'll afraid that's all we can do for now."

"I've got to get out of here. I want Clarkson and Fairthorpe. Both of them are no good and the longer they are free the more damage they'll do."

The doctor steps forward loading a hypodermic needle. "All right gentlemen you'll have to leave. Mr. Bobrowski needs rest now."

"I'm fine doctor. I don't need that needle. I'll just get up and give my leg some exercise."

"I can have an orderly here to restrain you while I administer this sedative if you insist. Your leg will not support your weight yet. I had to chase the bullet from the entry point at your knee to where it lodged in your upper thigh. You have more than thirty stitches that need time to heal the wound."

Clive gently pushes Reggie's shoulder back down to the bed. "Take it easy old chum; you'll only make it worse. We'll catch up to Clarkson soon enough. If you don't let that leg heal we won't make it to Tripoli."

Reggie relaxes his head back into the pillow. "Okay doctor, do your worst."

A day later, Reggie uses crutches to walk. Taking short trips through the hallways while watched closely by the doctor, he gains some mobility.

BOBO'S RAID

Nurses complain that Reggie roams the halls after the doctor leaves for the night. One night Reggie rounds a corner at a fast trot running into a nurse who juggles a bed pan furiously only to spill some of the contents on her uniform.

Exasperated with Reggie's exploits, the doctor orders him from the hospital and tells him to stay in the hotel and use the swimming pool for exercise. Using a cane to keep some weight off his leg, Reggie is soon back to work planning the mission. Using the Citroën's radio, he reports to number 10 Downing Street.

The London radio operator takes Reggie's information. The PM's message relayed to Reggie is that the new man taking over from the demise of Smyth will meet him and Clive in Tripoli. The PM assures this man is top-drawer.

The next week he and Clive fly to Tripoli with Nast and the German commander Schulz. Arriving at the airport Reggie and Clive follow the professor and Schulz through the customs station with little delay. As the men exit the customs queue, Alexandra and Fay rush past the two Germans. Nast and Schulz turn to watch with some bemused fascination as the women attack their husbands with hugs and kisses.

Reggie is almost toppled over. He grits his teeth and holds tightly to his cane.

"Bobo, oh Bobo, your poor leg," Ally cries.

Embarrassed at the outcry Reggie looks over Ally's shoulder to see the smile spread across Nast's face.

Reggie pulls Ally close to whisper in her ear, "Please Alexandra, you must stop calling me Bobo. See you later Professor. Perhaps we can get together for dinner."

Nast waves saying, "I will call you."

Alexandra clings to Reggie's free arm as they walk to the row of taxis.

"Look over there Reggie. Isn't that Marshal Balbo?"

They watch as the Governor-General of Libya by-passes German dignitaries to shake hands with the German racing drivers.

Ally whispers to Reggie, "I expected him to look more sinister. The magazines say he was a ruthless leader of the black shirts. He's really very dashing."

Marshal Balbo and several race drivers get into an Alfa Romeo sedan and drive away.

As they watch the big sedan leave, Reggie signals for a taxi. "Balbo may be a villain but his aircraft exploits are incredible. The people of Chicago named a street after him and President Roosevelt invited him to the White House to give him the Distinguished Flying Cross.

"He led an expedition of 24 flying boats from Rome to Chicago and back to Rome. That is some achievement. He's the ruler of Libya because Mussolini wants him away from Italy. Balbo could take Il Duce's place and he wants nothing to do with close ties to Germany. I read a quote from Balbo saying that siding with Germany would have Italy shining the Germans' shoes."

A little Fiat Balilla taxi pulls up. The driver rushes out to take their luggage from the porter. Clive hails another cab for him and Fay. A short ride from the airport brings them to a huge hotel overlooking the harbor. There are the usual small fishing boats bobbing alongside huge yachts on the sparkling water of the Mediterranean.

Clive and Fay's cab pulls up behind Reggie's cab. The men's luggage is quickly gathered by the hotel porters. Doors are held open as the two couples walk into the hotel lobby. The cavernous place is abuzz with people of all shapes and sizes. Arabs in beautifully embroidered flowing robes pass by. Italians, Europeans, men and women of every color bubble the air with excitement.

Clive with his head swiveling to take it all in says, "I say, old horse, this place shades Monte."

Fay and Ally grin at each other. "Wait till you see our rooms! The swimming pool is so elegant you want to wear a gown. They have a casino, too."

Fay excitingly adds, "We saw a man lose ten thousand pounds in a heartbeat at the roulette wheel." She pulls Clive close holding his hand. "But the best thing is spending some time with Clive away from the English winter."

Presenting their passports at the front desk, the desk clerk gives the men their room keys and a message for Reggie. He pockets the message and the couples head to the elevator.

After tipping the bell boy at their room, Reggie tears open the message. He steps back into the hallway and beckons Clive to join him.

"The PM's man is here. He wants to meet us in the bar at 8:00."

Entering the bar Reggie heads for a table in the corner of the sun-filled room. The ceiling fans whirl trying to beat back the day's heat. A man, seated with his back to the wall, has salt and pepper hair parted on the side and a thick mustache. A glass of what looks to be gin and tonic is on the table by an ashtray with a smoldering pipe resting on it.

Reggie stops at the man's table with his hand extended, "Reginald Bobrowski, and Clive Parry-Jones, at your service sir."

The man shakes their hands. "Charles Bayers here, please be seated gentlemen. Am I so obvious? Perhaps I should have a disguise of some sort."

Reggie sees the questioning look in Clive's face also before replying. "Not obvious sir, I was told to look for a proper gentleman. Your manner and Seville row suit are what sets you apart."

"I hope that is complimentary. I am not a man of the field in this job. An army officer in the last dust up, but behind a desk for too many years since."

Reggie lights a cigarette, the smoke curling up until the ceiling fans scatter it. "We are looking forward to your experience sir. The PM says you are first rate."

"Quite, quite. I am here to look into our two rogue agents. I do not wish to meddle into your assignment. I have spotted Clarkson here. I believe he and Fairthorpe are here to meet with their German handlers. We cannot legally arrest them in Libya. If I can get them back to Algeria, the French will hold them on robbery and assault charges.

"I want Claire Fairthorpe to stand trial for treason. We have proof she has passed our intelligence to the Germans. Clarkson is her lackey in all this. He is of small consequence to me. I may need to call upon you two for some assistance."

"We will be happy to oblige sir. I must say I am pleased Smyth is no longer in charge."

BOBO'S RAID

Bayers clears his throat, "Quite, quite, a nasty piece of work. The less said and all that."

Chapter 29

In a room on the ground floor of the same hotel, Claire Fairthorpe and Jenson Clarkson are drinking German beers.

"I almost ran into Bobo, your pretty boy snob, and his friends in the lobby. I thought I killed the bum in Ouargla. I could'a busted my leg jumpin' outta' that place."

Claire pulls Clarkson close to hiss in his ear. "Leave him alone, I won't tell you again. I need to find out what he knows."

Clarkson slaps her hand away. "Don't give me that crap. You think he found some mythical gold. That whole story's a bunch a hooey."

Claire looks surprised, then narrows her eyes to a hard stare. "Lay off him, or you're the one that's going to go mythical. Our German friends want Bobrowski alive for now."

"Lay off me sister. I've had it with you. I'm not takin' orders from you any more. You swish those hips and think every man in the world's gonna fall at your feet.

"You're not so smart. I may never be able to go back home again. You fouled that up good. You and your Mr. S.—the big deals, you're the smart ones. Well, I'll make my own deal with the krauts. I've done my fallin'. It'll be interestin' to see how long Olaf stays on your leash. He's big and dumb, but he thinks that gold story is real."

Claire puts her beer down on a table. "You're playing out of your league, Clarkson. I'm still in charge here; you'll do as I say."

Clarkson's eyes narrow, his back arches as if he is about to spring at her.

Claire suddenly has a pistol in her hand aimed at his head. "Sit down now! I won't hesitate to shoot you. You better hope the Germans have a use for you. That's the only reason you're alive. Drink your beer and cool off. I'm doing the meeting alone. I'll let you know what they say."

Reggie and Clive return to their rooms after the meeting with the new PM's man, Bayers. Alexandra wraps her arms around Reggie as soon as he enters the room. "I thought you were off on another adventure before we had one night together."

Reggie kisses her forehead. "Sorry love, it won't be all business I promise. Tonight belongs to us."

Late the next morning Reggie wobbles into the bathroom. He comes out of the bathroom to pull on undershorts and open the curtains to look out over the harbor. The sun gleams off the small waves, their tips sparkle like diamonds. Most of the working boats are out to the day's fishing. Large yachts with tall masts bob on the currents at their berths.

Ally yawns, then sits up and stretches in the bed. Reggie sits by her side. "Shall we have breakfast sent up, or would you prefer the restaurant?"

Ally kisses Reggie's cheek. "It's too beautiful to stay in the room all day. Let's knock up the Jones' and go to the restaurant for a big breakfast."

Pouring the last of the coffee into his cup, Reggie watches Ally and Fay wandering outside the restaurant through the colorful garden. He looks across the table at Clive. "Did you show Fay the pictures of Clarkson and Fairthorpe we got from Bayers?"

Clive nods. "The rogue's gallery you mean. Yes I did. I told her about them poisoning me to explain the bruises on my face. I'm afraid that's as much as I could say."

"Enjoy the time we have here Jonesy. It should be a wonderful week. The ladies are happy, the sun is bright, and I am anxious to see the new Grand Prix cars. However we should be vigilant about our spy friends. Both of them are nasty pieces of work. I don't want our problems with them to spill over to the women."

Ally and Fay return to the table bubbling over with the colors and textures of the exotic plants in the garden. "The pool looks lovely. Let's go up to our rooms and get our swim suits on."

"We just ate Ally; I thought we were supposed to wait an hour before going in the water."

"Oh come on Reg, the water will do your leg good. By the time we dress and order those fruit drinks, the hour will have flown by."

Clive rises from his chair. "Don't bother to argue old duck, water waits."

Fay moves to Clive's side. "I want to show Clive some post cards in the gift shop. We'll meet you at the pool. Okay?"

"Sure, see you there."

On the way to the elevator a man approaches Reggie. "Count, I understand you will not be driving this weekend. I am John Stengel; I have a perfectly marvelous Maser I would like you to drive at Donington this year."

Reggie turns to his wife, "Ally why don't you go on up, I'll be there in a jiff."

Alexandra smiles and enters the elevator.

Leaving the elevator on her floor Ally walks toward her room. A man turns in the hallway and walks toward her. She nods and smiles as the man passes, then stops as she recognizes the man from the pictures Reggie showed her.

She turns back to warn Reggie. Clarkson stops at the stairwell hearing Ally coming behind him. Ally moves to the other side of the hallway hoping to get past.

Clarkson moves to block her way. "I see you know who I am. I know who you are."

Ally stands her ground. "I don't know what you mean sir. I'm on my way back to the restaurant. I think forgot my lighter on the table."

Clarkson grabs Ally by the shoulders and shoves her against the wall by the stairs. Her head strikes the wall with dull thud making her cry out.

Reggie exits the elevator from behind Clarkson to see him attack Ally. Rising his cane he chops down on Clarkson's head with all the force in his arm. The heavy cane goes down the side of Clarkson's head tearing his ear. He screams grabbing his ear and tumbles down the stairs to the landing.

Ally pulls Reggie to her, "Don't go after him. You can't go down the stairs on your bad leg."

Clarkson gets up off the floor, blood seeping under the hand over his ear. "You bastard. I'll kill you for this."

Reggie yells back from the head of the stairs. "You will be the one dead if you come near my wife again. You won't catch me without my pistol again. I am going to report this assault to the police here. You're going to run out of countries to hide from warrants."

Clarkson gets a pistol unsnagged from his pocket. Reggie pushes Ally around the corner and goes to their room to get his gun.

Once in the room Ally rushes for the phone to call the front desk. She reports that a man with a gun assaulted her. Putting her hand over the phone's mouthpiece, she calls to Reggie. "Reginald do not go after him. Let the hotel or the police do their jobs. You can't run after him anyway. I'll call the gift shop and warn Clive and Fay."

Ally turns away from Reggie to hide her sudden stream of tears. She is uncertain if hitting her head in the attack, or fear for their lives, is the cause of the outburst.

Reggie takes the moment to grab his pistol and slip out the door.

Chapter 30

Pulling the door shut as quietly as possible Reggie turns his key to lock the door. After scanning both ends of the hallway to make sure Clarkson didn't come after them, he moves to the stairwell. "Cursed cane," Reggie mutters under his breath. With the cane in his right hand supporting him, holding the big Colt pistol in his left hand feels unnatural.

At the stairwell he switches the pistol to his right hand and carefully looks around the corner. He sees no sign of Clarkson.

There are sounds of men coming up the stairwell. Reggie stays at the corner to make sure the men are not herding Clarkson back up the stairs. As the first hotel man appears Reggie pockets his pistol and heads back to his room.

Ally hugs Reggie fiercely when he comes into the room. Tears streak down her cheeks. "I couldn't find my room key to unlock the door. Please stay with me. My head hurts and I'd like to lie down, but I'm afraid you'll leave."

"Go lie down sweetheart. I'll get an aspirin and a cool towel for your head. I expect the police will be here soon. If you feel up to it later, we'll go down to the pool."

Ally turns to go to the bedroom, "Will you stay here?"

"I'll stay right here, don't worry. I don't think Clarkson will try anything else today. He'll need to take care of that ear. He's losing a lot of blood."

Reggie opens the door when the police arrive to question him about Clarkson's attack. Reggie gives a detailed description of Clarkson and explains to the Italian policeman that Clarkson is wanted in Algeria for robbery and assault.

"Yes, yes," The policeman says, "but what has that to do with the assault on your wife here?"

The policeman watches enviously as Reggie opens a pack of American cigarettes. Reggie taps a cigarette from the pack and offers one to the policeman. The man takes the cigarette and puffs appreciatively as Reggie lights it for him.

"Clarkson shot me in Ouargla making his getaway. I think he attacked my wife trying to get at me. He may be trying to eliminate me as a witness. At the rate he's losing blood I hope it will be easy for you to find him."

The Italian speaks, exhaling twin streams of smoke from his nostrils. "If he seeks help with his injuries here in the city, we will have him. However he could be long away."

Reggie opens the room's door to usher the men out. "I hope you find him. Be careful, the man's a crack shot."

In the early afternoon Clive and Fay tap on the door. Reggie opens the door to see them with a steward who has a meal cart. The steward pushes the cart carrying a large silver bowl filled with ice and bottles of beer into the room. After the steward leaves Clive pulls a bottle from the ice. "I say, old Yank, we thought cold beer would be just the thing."

BOBO'S RAID

Reggie takes the proffered bottle. "Spot on, old bean."

Ally comes out of the bedroom brushing her hair. "Cold beer! What a marvelous treat. Reggie, would you open one for me dear?"

The beer is soon consumed. Ally holds some ice in a napkin to her forehead. "I feel much better. Let's go down to the pool. The afternoons are quite warm here. Floating on the water will be just the ticket."

Reggie holds on to the edge of the pool and gently pumps his legs in the cool water. Stitchwork snakes up his leg; his knee is still red and swollen. Bending the knee more than a few degrees brings shooting pain to the joint.

A shadow moves over Reggie's head. Raising his head to look up, Reggie sees a man wearing a military uniform. His polished visor cap has an elaborately embroidered band indicating a person of importance.

"Count Bobrowski? I am Italo Balbo, Governor-General of Libya. May I have a word with you?"

"Yes sir, I am at your service Governor-General. I'll be with you in a moment."

Reggie breast stokes to the shallow end of the pool. He uses the handrail on the gentle stairs as support to exit the pool. Ally rises from her lounge chair to bring his cane, and help him slip on a terry cloth robe.

The two men shake hands and take seats across from each other at a table shaded by a large red and blue Cinzano umbrella. A waiter appears to place a pitcher of ice water and two glasses on the table and fades away.

"I have a police report of an attack on you and your wife by a wanted criminal. I was not aware of your presence here. The latest entry list has you scratched due to injury. I have directed the police to do all possible to apprehend the man."

"Thank you, sir. My wife and I are much obliged. I had no idea the man would follow me from Algeria. I wanted to see the world's fastest race circuit and race here but I can't move my knee enough to be any good."

Marshal Balbo wipes the headband of his cap with a handkerchief. "I have a lovely Alfa 8C. Would you care to accompany me for a tour of the course? I do enjoy showing the place off."

"I would be honored. I had a Maserati to race but cancelled it. The Germans tell me no car can match their cars."

Balbo fits his cap back on his head. "Yes, the Germans. They are like a steam roller. Their cars are fastest to be sure. In this depression's economy the money they spend is amazing. Ah well, I still love the sound of my Alfa at full chat. By the way, I read an article about you modifying a Citroën to use as a military vehicle. Is it good in deep sand?"

Reggie sips cold water from a glass that feels cool and wet in his hand. Putting the glass on the table, he rolls the glass between his hands as he answers. "The Citroën was strong enough to rescue the German's big cargo trucks that were stuck in the sand in Algeria. My partner and I have modified the Citroën with more power and traction than the factory model. We have better tracks for the sands and more cargo space. We can armor plate the cab and the cargo box. Our truck can be used as a goods carrier, a personnel transport, or a gun platform.

"It's a nimble, fast, and dependable vehicle that can pack a good punch if so outfitted. We have not had a failure of any kind with it to date."

Marshal Balbo grins, his teeth flash white between his black mustache and goatee. "That is quite an endorsement Count. We will talk more of this. The morning will be cool, a good time to tour the racetrack. I will send a car for you and your companions at 8 o'clock. I must get back to my duties. It is a pleasure to meet you, Count."

"The pleasure is all mine sir. We will be ready tomorrow morning. Thank you for your generosity."

Chapter 31

Reggie and Ally have breakfast overlooking the harbor. The water in the harbor is light blue, smooth and quiet. Men with their fishing boats were out early in search of the day's pay.

Ally sips the last of her coffee. Leaning back in her chair she stretches bringing her hands above her head. "I love having breakfast out here on the balcony. The air is still cool and the harbor is beautiful. Spending time here in the winter could become a habit."

Reggie wipes away crumbs from his toast with a napkin. "Did your family go to Florida every winter dear?"

"My mother and I did. Father would sometimes have to work at his bank, but he would come down for some weekends. Florida was wide open then. Not many people and lots of open land. The beaches were fantastic. The bad part was all the insects. You could get eaten alive. But as a child it was a grand adventure."

Reggie snaps his fingers. "That reminds me, I must find some more of those colorful golf caps."

"Oh my gosh, now I wish I'd have kept my mouth shut. I'd rather see you in a, a, I don't know. Well anything, a turban would be better."

Chuckling Reggie pushes back his chair. "Let's get going. The car Marshal Balbo is sending for us should be here soon."

BOBO'S RAID

The doors to the elevator hiss open to let Reggie and Ally step out into the lobby. Clive and Fay are there waiting to greet them.

Clive, in a cheery mood, claps Reggie on the back. "Morning, old darlings. Balbo's man is here to take us out to the track."

Reggie flicks his lighter to fire up his first cigarette of the day. "You're mighty chipper this morning, old fellow."

Putting his arm around Fay's waist Clive smiles back at Reggie. "I think it must be the warm sea air, old salt. Could be something to do with the company I keep." He winks at Fay.

"I am looking forward to the race. I needn't worry about your driving; I can just enjoy the race. I may even place a wager after practice, then back to the hotel pool and cocktails. This is the life, old count."

It is a short ride to the race track. The car pulls up behind a huge dazzling white tower. Stepping around from his place behind the steering wheel, the driver opens the rear door and says, "Please go through the tower. Governor-General Balbo has his cars in the garages. He is waiting for you there."

The couples walk though the tower's entranceway. Polished marble floors and elegant columns mark the beautiful interior of the building. Outside across the track is a modern white canopied grandstand stretching down the straight. The massive grandstand has seating for tens of thousands.

Clive tilts his head back to look up at the outside of the tower building. "I've not seen the likes of this since we were in Indianapolis. This is fantastic. The lottery must bring in millions of lira."

Down the row of garages, a car engine starts. Marshal Balbo, wearing a cloth helmet, is walking toward the couples, pulling on his driving gloves. "Are you ready Count?"

"Ready as I'll ever be. Your Alfa sounds good, it is a beautiful car."

The blood-red Alfa rumbles onto the tarmac. A mechanic straps closed the engine cover as the men get in the car. Reggie struggles some to get his bad leg positioned in the car.

Balbo pulls out of the pits, the engine howls and by the time he shifts to third gear they are out on the track at full throttle.

Clive, Ally, and Fay rush to the pit wall to watch. Clouds of dust, and sand billow up to follow behind the car as the Alfa disappears into the simmering haze of heat rising from the tarmac.

Supercharger whine and blaring exhaust echo back to the pits as the car is hurled round the circuit. The Marshal is not wasting any time getting around. After four laps of the circuit the car appears at the entrance to the pits, both men are smiling and gesturing with their hands. The Alfa stops by Reggie's wife and friends.

"Who's next?" the Marshal roars over the cars' loud exhaust.

Clive steps forward and Reggie opens the car's door for him. "Enjoy old chum. He'll give you a good go."

The Alfa squats down, black smoke belching from the exhaust, as Balbo tears out of the pits.

Cars and crews are appearing from the garages. The crews begin to set up their equipment by their pit. The first practice for the Grand Prix is ready to start as soon as Balbo finishes his laps. A man comes out of the tower building with a checkered flag to signal Balbo the finish of his laps.

Balbo flashes by waving his hand to acknowledge the flagman.

Stopping by Reggie's group Balbo shouts an invitation to a party he is giving as Clive climbs from the car. Reggie shouts back, "We'll be there, thanks for the laps."

Balbo salutes the group and roars down to the end of the garages.

After watching the first practice Ally suggests they return to the hotel to cool off with a swim in the pool.

Reggie slides down in the cool water of the hotel's pool. Ally joins him at the shallow end of the pool, her long blond hair now wet and slicked back.

"Sit down on the step and I'll massage your leg while you do your bending exercises."

Reggie grimaces trying to pull his knee to his chest. "I know now there was no chance of driving here. Just getting thrown around in Balbo's Alfa was painful. Your hands feel good Ally, I think I'll live."

Clive and Fay splash in the water, playing like children. They soon tire of the water and join Ally and Reggie at a table, sipping fruit drinks.

Reggie is facing Ally and notices her head slightly tremble. She looks at Reggie her brows knitted. "What's wrong Ally?" Standing up from her chair she looks from side to side; turning around she looks behind her. "I've got shivers running up my back. I have the strangest feeling someone is watching us."

Clarkson yanks the binoculars from his eyes and ducks down behind the ledge of the roof. Crouching behind the ledge he feels silly. There is no way the woman could have spotted him. She could not possibly know what he is planning.

Chapter 32

Reggie sits out on the balcony with Ally having breakfast, his face buried in a newspaper. Ally steals the last pieces of toast and is spreading jam on a piece when Reggie reaches out to find an empty plate.

Reggie peers over the paper. Ally smiles mischievously. "Snooze you lose."

"Why you little pirate, stealing the last of my toast," Reggie pouts. "On the high seas that could earn you forty lashes. The last piece is always the best."

Nibbling the piece she put jam on she says, "My, oh my, forty lashes, what a brute you are. Here you can have very last piece. I didn't think you'd notice. You were lost in the newspaper."

"I see, just punishment for my inattention then. The paper has an article about Nuvolari having a shunt yesterday. Apparently a tire blew on his Alfa and threw him out of the car. He broke some ribs and the doctors have forbidden him to race.

"I doubt the doctors will have the last word. I want to go out to some of the corners today and watch. The Merc's don't seem to be as fast as the Auto-Unions here. I wonder if it's going to be Audi's year this year. Are you ready to go?"

"I need to brush my teeth first, Captain Bly."

Getting up from the table a flash of sunlight catches his eye. Looking up he scans the direction of where he thinks the light came from, but doesn't see anything.

When they arrive at the race track, Fay and Ally decide to watch from the comfort of the tower. Reggie and Clive head out to the infield to watch. The race cars kick up huge clouds of sand as they rip around the turns. The sand blows across the tarmac faster than the cars can disperse it, sandblasting the fronts of cars that closely follow each other. Within a few laps the paint and bright work are worn away.

Walking miles through the inside of the race course the two men stop at a turn shaded by palm trees. Standing only a few feet inside one of the fast turns Reggie watches Hans Stuck fly by at almost 180 miles an hour. Stuck, with the car in a four wheel drift, commits to the corner. Steering with slight movements of the big steering wheel, he rockets past.

Clive wipes a handkerchief across his face. "It's getting warmish, old camel. What say we head back for a drink? I know the bloke I'm putting a fiver on. That boy Rosemeyer is more than the rest of the chasers can handle. My watch has him two or three seconds a lap faster than anyone else."

"Righto, we'll pick up the ladies at the tower and be off."

Balbo's party that night is lavish. Champagne flows like water. Fish, pasta, and lamb are served by beautiful ladies garbed in flowing Berber dress. Music is provided by an American jazz band. Drivers and their wives are the center of attention for much of the evening. Balbo is busy most of the evening shaking hands and making small talk.

BOBO'S RAID

Reggie with Ally on his arm makes the rounds talking to the racers they know. Reggie introduces Ally to Professor Nast. Much of the talk is about whether Nuvolari will obey the doctors or race his Alfa.

Balbo, resplendent in his uniform approaches, bows to Reggie and kisses Ally's hand.

"Count, I would like to talk to you about your caterpillar. The Germans are most impressed by your vehicle. I was just speaking to Professor Nast; he gives you very high marks. He said you made pulling their trucks from the sand look easily done. We must meet to look at the specifications and prices of your desert roamer."

Reggie is genuinely pleased. "I would be delighted to discuss the matter with you sir. I am at your service."

"Can you be available after the race? Say Monday afternoon?"

"I'm honored Governor-General. Yes that will be fine, thank you."

"I will have my office contact you for the appointment. I look forward to driving one of your trucks."

Reggie turns to Ally. "That was more than I expected. If we can sell trucks to Balbo, we are on our way. You always bring me good luck, my sweet pirate."

Ally looks up into Reggie eyes. "Sell your truck to Balbo and come home with me. Don't go back to Algeria. I worry so when I'm not with you."

"I have to finish the mission for the PM. It won't be long Ally. Nast is going to Tamanrasset as the end of their expedition. Jonesy and I will follow from a distance and that will end our commitment also. You and Fay can stay here and soak up the sun for a few more days if you like. It will take me two or three more weeks in Algeria and we'll all be home to enjoy spring together.

"Don't worry love, let's have another dance and we'll be off. Nast would like us to have breakfast with him tomorrow. We can watch the race and be back at the hotel in the pool before dinner."

"Somehow," Ally says, "that doesn't keep me from being worried."

Most of the race team members have finished breakfast by the time Ally and Reggie meet Professor Nast in the hotel restaurant. The ceiling fans are working hard to clear the room of the cigarette smoke swirling around the whirling blades. As soon as they are seated a waiter brings fresh coffee to their table.

Nast is at his best recounting stories of Reggie's father and their adventures together. Ally's mood is lightened and she is soon dabbing tears of laughter from her eyes. "Please have mercy Professor. I'm not sure my sides can take much more laughing. I never met Reggie's father. I somehow think of him as being a staunch man. I can see now where Reggie gets his sense of humor."

After breakfast, Nast gives Reggie and Ally a hair-raising ride in his car out to the racetrack. Mashing the horn and darting in and out of traffic, the Professor drives like a man possessed. Ally squeezes Reggie's hand for the duration of the wild ride to the racetrack.

Professor Nast bids Ally and Reggie a hasty adieu and is off through the crowd to his place at the German viewing stand.

BOBO'S RAID

"Whew," Ally expels a deep breath. "I wondered if we were going to get here in one piece. That guy drives like a maniac. I'm glad we have some seats reserved."

Ally clings to Reggie's arm as they move amongst the crowd. They have to steer against the tide of people to get into the tower.

Inside the tower Ally searches for Clive and Fay. "I've never seen so many people. It's almost frightening. You'd be crushed if you stumbled and fell."

Marshal Balbo reviews the drivers and cars in a ceremony before the start of the race. Nuvolari is there with his ribs taped up and a spare Alfa Romeo ready for him.

The cars roar off from a standing start. The Auto-Unions and Mercedes cars are in a race of their own. With over 500-horsepower, and capable of 200-mile an hour speeds, the German factory cars soon leave the Alfa's and Maserati's in the dust.

Rosemeyer retires with a fuel fire in his Auto Union. Clive rips his betting slip into little pieces in disgust. The race is not without drama. The Mercedes cars are in trouble early. Rudi Caracciola and Luigi Fagioli have both lost the front brakes and are dropping back. Hans Stuck opens up a good lead in his Auto Union. He looks set for a well-earned Grand Prix win. That is until Dr. Feuereissen, the new Auto Union team manager, signals Stuck to slow down.

The German team managers have been told that an Italian should win the race if at all possible. Each time Stuck passes the pits he is signaled to slow down. Now Stuck's Auto Union teammate, Italian Achille Varzi, is signaled to speed up. The gap Stuck opened up to his teammate closes. On the last lap, Varzi breaks the lap record to pass a very surprised Hans Stuck.

Most of the Italian contingent are overjoyed. However not everyone is pleased with the outcome. The 1933 Tripoli Grand Prix went down in history as a "fixed" race. The huge crowd sitting in the grandstands and the tower were in full view of the strange signaling the Auto Union team manager was performing. It was obvious this race would also be recorded as a "fixed" race.

Chapter 33

Marshal Balbo throws a huge victory party after the race. Reggie, Clive and their wives are all enjoying the festivities. The large room has a terrace looking out over the twinkling lights of the harbor. The walls reverberate with the sounds of laughter. Voices rise in exclamation with tales of the day's racing adventures. In one end of the room, Hans Stuck delights a group of people with a demonstration of his alpine yodeling.

Balbo, at the head of the room, clinks his glass and calls for silence.

"Let us toast the men of today's Grand Prix."

The men and women raise their glasses. Balbo raises his glass. "I toast Hans Stuck, today's real winner."

A murmur goes through the crowd. Ally's face takes on a look of confusion as she looks at Reggie. Reggie smiles at her and raises his glass. From the terrace comes the sound of breaking glass. Achille Varzi, the man who crossed the finish line first, feels humiliated and, in a fit of anger, he throws down his glass and storms out and down the stairs.

Varzi's exit seems to spell an end to the evening's celebrations. On their way out, Marshal Balbo asks Reggie to come into another room to make an appointment with his secretary. Upon entering the room Balbo introduces Reggie to a small-statured man who shakes Reggie's hand and returns to his seat behind a huge ornate desk.

Balbo stands to the side of the desk. "Would the afternoon suit you Count? I think we could all do with a good night's rest."

Reggie nods his head in affirmation. "Yes sir, that would be fine."

On the cab ride back to their hotel, the couples decide to have a drink at the bar before turning in for the night.

Reggie leads the way to the hotel's bar. "It's really too early for bed. We should have our own celebration. It's been lovely to visit with the ladies, and we have a good sales lead with Balbo. If we can convince Balbo to buy one of our Citroëns, Algeria will be a success."

"I'll toast to that," Clive chimes in. "I'm all for a quick end to our desert roaming, old Arab. Spring in England, is there anywhere more beautiful?" Clive looks around the room, and lowers his voice conspiratorially. "How much longer will we have to be following the Jerrys, do you think?"

Reggie puts his finger to his lips to signal quiet. "We have to go on to Tamanrasset and it's a long trip." Reggie puts his hand up to stop further discussion. "I know, I know, but we have to finish this. As soon as we're done, I promise I'll charter a plane to take us home."

Clive pats Fay's hand. "I'm with you, old man, let's change the subject. What was Balbo on about with that toast to Hans Stuck? He certainly surprised Varzi. The man turned four shades of red before he stormed away."

BOBO'S RAID

Fay glances at Ally. "We hear he's playing around with another man's wife. The Italian newspapers have hinted about it. The woman in question is supposed to be a drug addict according to the press."

Clive falls silent drawing into himself. Reggie quickly changes the course of the conversation. "Well, we all know the way of newsprint, especially the Italian newspapers. Anyway, to get back to Balbo, I think he's a mischief maker. The toast to Stuck was done for effect. Maybe he didn't like the way the Auto Union team manager was so obvious about it. It's his big event and, for the second time, the fix was in."

Ally stifles a yawn as they finish their bottle of champagne. "I'm all in. It's been a long day. Breakfast together on the balcony of our room would be lovely. Fay and I are going to have our hair done while you two are meeting with Marshal Balbo."

Jenson Clarkson, from his vantage point on the hotel's roof, sees the lights go off in Reggie's room. After watching for his chance to even the score, he hopes that Monday morning will be the day he has waited for.

Chapter 34

Looking at his reflection in the tarnished mirror Clarkson saw his swollen face. The torn ear he received from Reggie's cane had become infected. He found a so-called doctor to re-attach his flapping ear. After enduring the pain of the stitching on his ear, Clarkson paid an outrageous sum for the doctor's silence. Afraid of the police finding him at his hotel, Jenson found a cheap room.

Exhausted he fell asleep on the bed as soon as he got into the room. In the morning's light he found the flea-bag room was, indeed, flea infested. Clarkson swallowed some aspirin and gritted his teeth as he poured alcohol over his ear. As soon as the liquid hit it stung like blazes. Jenson bit down on his hand to keep from screaming. His anger at Claire Fairthorpe's wanting nothing to do with him anymore stung also.

They met in Monaco three years ago. Clarkson's grandmother died leaving him 40 thousand pounds. Jenson's father disgraced the family name by embezzling money from the insurance company he worked for. Young and handsome, Clarkson took his inheritance and fled England.

Claire was magic in Monaco. She bewitched Jenson. They had a wild affair. Together they travelled the Mediterranean countries in the lap of luxury before he ran out of money in Algeria. He was left with his hopped-up model A Ford and a broken heart. Claire had used him up and he knew it. He still thought he loved her.

Claire offered him a job. They would be spies together. The money was good and she promised him a life filled with excitement like he had never known. Instead she ran him like a dog on a leash.

If he tried to leave, she threatened to turn him in as a traitor. She flaunted her practice of sleeping with anyone she needed to do her bidding. He knew she was evil but that was what always excited him about her.

Clarkson looks in the mirror at his ruined face. His hand bleeds from where he bit it. Touching his ear he begins to talk to himself. "You son of a bitch you destroyed my face. I'll kill you Bobrowski and maybe I'll kill Claire too.

"I hate that pompous bastard. From the first time I saw him I hated him. He thinks he's too good for Claire; maybe I hate him a little for that. She still wants him alive. Well I'm going to kill him havin' breakfast on that lovely balcony. I'll get that scoped Mauser out of Claire's car and splatter his brains all over that pretty little wife of his. Hell, maybe I'll kill her too."

Pulling on a hooded Arab robe, Clarkson leaves the flea-bag room. He always has a sense of satisfaction when his model A fires up. When he had money he sent away to America to get the Miller overhead cam cylinder head. The cream-colored Ford was fast and the last of his possessions he had not lost to his lust for Claire.

Chapter 35

At a posh hotel inland from the harbor Claire Fairthorpe pulls away from the outstretched arm of the fat man on her bed. A sheen of sweat still covers his body. She is grateful the man is snoring in spurts, still asleep. Her Nazi handlers, who once praised her spy craft, were not pleased with the Mr. S affair. They lost a valuable source of information. Fairthorpe had not warned them of any problems. So now she had to sleep with fat old men the Nazis wanted to blackmail.

Washing herself with a wet cloth she looks away from the mirror above the basin. Donning a robe she walks into the other room. On the way, she gathers her cigarettes and opens the curtains to the French doors. Palm trees sway gently in the morning breeze. The alley below is wide and uncluttered. Across the alley is the hotel's car park.

Stepping out on the balcony Claire lights her cigarette taking the smoke deep in her lungs. The taste of the harsh tobacco helps to rid her mind of the thoughts of the man in her bed. She thinks of packing her bags and driving away. Looking down to find her car in the lot, she sees a man stop behind the car. He has a crowbar and is wrenching the trunk lid open.

She chokes off the scream in her throat not wanting to draw any attention to her car. Pulling on a sun dress she races out of the room. Not wasting time with the elevator she runs down three flights of stairs to burst out of the rear door of the hotel running to her car. No one is around but the trunk lid's lock is mangled. Lifting the trunk lid Claire finds the wooden shelf Clarkson made to hide the guns askew.

Claire quickly scans her surroundings before lifting the wood. It only takes her a second to realize the scoped Mauser is gone. In the same instant she knows who took the rifle and why.

Jenson fashioned a turban on his head that covered his ears. The hood would no longer be a hindrance to his ability to sight the rifle. Getting the rifle was easier than he expected. He had a pocket full of sharp nosed 8-millimeter bullets. Jouncing over the rough road on the outskirts of Tripoli he looked for a secluded place that he could sight in the rifle.

The desert was very still and empty, most of the population was at the racetrack. Clarkson knows the distance from the hotel rooftop to Bobrowski's balcony is slightly less than 100 yards. He finds a rise in the desert that approximates the down angle of the shot he will make.

Setting up a wood plank, he goes back up the hill, lies prone on the soft sand and sights the rifle. The first shot throws up sand a few feet short and to the right of the plank. Clarkson adjusts the windage and elevation knobs on the scope. Four more rounds give him the accuracy he wants. Laying the rifle down on a blanket, Jenson goes back to his car.

On the passenger side floor of his model A is an object wrapped in paper. Clarkson picks up the object and heads back to the place he put the wood plank. At the plank Jenson unwraps the paper and puts a goat's head in front of the plank. Back on top of the rise he sights through the rifle's scope, takes a breath and holds it.

Gently squeezing the trigger the rifle bucks hard into his shoulder. The goats head literally disintegrates. A cloud of red dust splatters against the plank. Clarkson feels some elation. The real shot at Bobrowski's hotel should be easy. Back at his car he carefully cleans the rifle before heading back to Tripoli.

Monday morning Clarkson is on the hotel rooftop, the sun already hot on his back. Around 8:30 the balcony door to Bobrowski's room opens. A waiter wheels a food cart out before him. With a practiced flourish the man snaps a tablecloth and places it on the table top. Placing the plates and silverware on the table first, he brings the silver-domed food platters from inside the cart. Checking the table to be certain everything is in place, the waiter goes back into the room pushing the cart.

Ally and Fay are the first two people to appear. Clarkson brings the rifle up and sets it on the roof's ledge. The women are pouring coffee into cups and beckoning the men to the table. Clarkson pulls the rifle stock to his cheek. Two men come out on the balcony. Clive sits with his back to Clarkson. Reggie sits across from Clive.

Claire Fairthorpe rushes back to her room to get her Walther pistol specially equipped with a silencer. The fat man rises from the bed and grabs her wrist. "Come back to bed my sweet little dumpling, I am ready for you again."

Claire yanks her wrist from his grip and takes the pistol from a dresser drawer. Turning back toward the man Claire points the pistol at him. "Do not be here when I return, you fill me with disgust."

He puts his hands up defensively and turns away. Claire grabs her purse and rushes from the room.

She spends the day looking for Clarkson in every place she can think of. She knows her handlers will not forgive another mistake. The day passes without any sign of Clarkson. Late into the night she prowls from bar to bar in hope of catching a drunken Clarkson off guard. Tired, her throat sore from yelling at drunks and too many cigarettes, she drags back to her hotel.

Claire tosses and turns restlessly, sleep only comes in fits. With the sun just coming up, she suddenly throws the covers off and bolts out of bed. At the cab stand in front of her hotel she steps in front of a couple and slams the door closed. She yells at the cab driver, "Get me to the Harbor Hotel now!"

Throwing money to the driver when they arrive at the hotel she rushes from the cab. Facing the front of the hotel she sees two wings of the building that jut out from the center rooms. She knows where Bobrowski's room is, but now must decide which of the wings Clarkson would choose. She runs to her right.

On the rooftop Clarkson mutters, "Son of a bitch." Clive's head is in the way of his shot. Clarkson takes the rifle down and moves further out to his right. The shot will have to be at an angle he did not foresee. Laying the rifle on the ledge he puts a blanket down to kneel on. Looking through the scope he brings the center of the crosshairs to bear on the left side of Reggie's head.

Claire reaches the rooftop of the building's wing. Opening the door to the roof slowly, she looks through the gap. Not seeing anyone she goes through the door. The roof is empty; no one is at the ledge overlooking the rooms below. "Damn it! Wrong wing." Fairthorpe runs back to the door.

Out on the balcony, Ally and Fay are putting the food on plates and setting the plates before the men. Clarkson waits for the women to sit down. With the women settled he pulls the rifle's stock into his shoulder and sights through the scope. Ally's head is just forward, bending toward her food. Reggie's head is perfectly in the crosshairs. Clarkson takes a deep breath.

Clarkson suddenly stiffens with pressure of a gun barrel pressed into the back of his neck. "Put the rifle down Jenson. I told you not to go after Bobrowski."

Clarkson slides the rifle down from the ledge. "How the hell did you find me?"

Clarkson tries to turn to see Claire. The pistol barrel digs harder into his neck. "Stay just where you are. Don't move."

The silenced pistol bucks in her hand, Clarkson's body slumps forward resting on the ledge. Claire puts her pistol down to go through his pockets for any identification, then lifts Clarkson's feet. His body slides over the ledge and down the side of the building. At the second story of the building, the body strikes a metal awning. Upon striking the awning his lifeless arms spring out like wings as he flies out away from the side of the building. His body hits the street below head first, his skull mushrooming out like a burst melon.

Claire wipes the rifle of any finger prints and wraps it in the blanket. Looking for a place to hide the gun she spots a water tank in a corner of the building's wing.

BOBO'S RAID

Lifting the lid of the water tank, she unwraps the rifle from the blanket and drops it in. She does not want the blanket to stop up the water flow and lead to the detection of the rifle. Outside the hotel's rear entrance, she puts the blanket under other refuse in a trash can. A woman screams at the front of the hotel as she walks away.

Chapter 36

The commotion on the street below the breakfasting couples goes largely unnoticed. At one point, Clive gets up to look over the balconies railing. "I can't see much, just a group of people on the street standing around down there. Maybe one of those crazy cab drivers hit someone."

The rest of the day goes by in a blur of activity. Clive and Reggie meet with Marshal Balbo. The meeting is short and to the point.

Walking from out of Balbo's office Reggie hands Clive his briefcase while he unbuttons his sport coat. Clive hands him the briefcase back adding, "I can't believe that was so easy. He really wants our Citroën. When you suggested he could have his men pick it up in Tamanrasset he was all for it. Bloody good show, old fox."

"Jonesy, old fellow, I'm happy too. It'll knock a week or so off the time for us to get home. We need to get in touch with Professor Nast to see when his plane leaves tomorrow. Let's go to the ticket office and get Fay and Ally a nice ship to Italy and plane tickets home from there. We'll do our own celebrating tonight."

Early morning dust devils swirl on the tarmac. The runways of the Tripoli airport are black ribbons running through the sands with white lines painted down the center. Ally and Fay, their eyes bright but tearful, wave at the silver plane lifting its nose into the sky.

Professor Nast gets up out of his seat as soon as the plane levels out at cruising altitude. He beckons Reggie and Clive to follow him to the rear of the plane. "Have a seat at the table gentlemen. I will make coffee."

Measuring coffee into a Krupp electric peculator, he secures it to a small counter and takes a seat at the table. "The thought of that shameful Grand Prix display still upsets me. Hans Stuck won that race, even Balbo said so. I know there are team orders, but they usually discuss them before the race. To flag Hans down in front of a hundred thousand people just boils my blood."

"I would like," Reggie says, "to see the Mercs and Audis have some competition."

Nast places cups on the table. "You're forgetting Nuvolari gets a win every now and then. Mercedes brought in Dick Seaman to please you English. I understand Neubauer is testing an American Indy car man."

Reggie and Clive trade puzzled looks. Reggie asks, "Who's the Indy car guy, Professor?"

"I believe his name is Novac, Jack Novac. The German sports director and I were just talking about him this weekend. My information is that Neubauer is very impressed with the man."

"That's the man," Reggie says. "If any of those American cowboys could make it in a Grand Prix car, Novac would be the man."

Nast looks surprised. "You know this Novac?"

"Oh yeah," Reggie replies. "He's got quite a reputation as a practical joker. But from what Jonesy and I have seen the man is naturally fast and very determined. It's been pretty widely reported that the young drivers Neubauer tested wrecked a lot of cars. Novac's a pro. I imagine he would look good after the amateurs Neubauer's run."

"I could talk to my friend the sports director to see if we could get you a test drive."

"Professor, I'd give my eye teeth to drive one of your Grand Prix cars, but I don't want to be a professional driver. I like to pick and choose my drives, and I have no bosses."

"Are you sure it is not politics you find untenable?"

"I respect you Professor so I won't lie. I find the Nazi propaganda very disturbing. I believe I know you and know that you are a good man. I am worried that Hitler and his…gang are up to no good. But I would still love to drive one of those cars just one time."

Commander Schulz moves past the table to pour himself a cup of coffee. He stops at the table on his way back to his seat. Leaning over the professor's shoulder he speaks in a low voice. "Political discussions are best left to places that are more private." He nods toward two men seated at the front of the plane.

The professor, unseen by the commander, rolls his eyes. "Yes of course commander. You are, I am sure, quite right."

After the commander is back in his seat Reggie leans forward in his chair. "Can we have dinner in Ouargla Professor? It may be a long time before we're able to enjoy your company again."

"Dinner sounds fine Count. What time would you like to meet?"

BOBO'S RAID

"By the time we get back to the hotel and do some catching up it will be dinnertime. Jonesy and I have to check out our Citroën and stock some provisions, but that will probably take a day or two. Why don't we meet at my room about 8 o'clock? The three of us can have an enjoyable dinner in the room with no listeners."

Nast leans forward across the table and says in a low voice, "Good. You know in my country they say you must look both ways before you speak these days."

Sand and dust billow up behind the wheels of the plane as it touches down on the hard-packed dirt runway. Taxiing by a grove of date palms the pilot shuts down the plane's engines. The two men who sat in the front of the plane hustle the commander and Professor Nast into a waiting car and drive off.

Clive turns to Reggie, "Well, old outcast, I guess we need to find our own way to the hotel."

Reggie picks up his bags and starts toward the city. "Come on Jonesy, we've got a lot to do before dinner tonight."

Walking through the dusty streets, some blocks are almost deserted, others are a beehive of activity. The two men dodge in and out of children playing, dogs barking, vender's wooden-wheeled carts, and women carrying mountains of dates perched on their heads. Clive stops at a corner, hopping on one foot trying to get a pebble out of his shoe. "Who do you think those two rough looking fellows were on the plane with us?"

Reggie reaches out to hold on to Jonesy keeping him from tipping over. "I would say Gestapo. I can only guess why they're here. We can ask the professor tonight. I don't know if he can tell us anything or not."

Clive and Reggie, tired from their walk, drink two cold beers in the hotel bar. The outside of the glass mugs bead with cool condensation. Clive rolls the mug across his forehead. "It's getting too hot for me old boy. I'd like to think we'll be done with this soon."

"The professor is as weary of the desert as you are my friend. The journey to Tamanrasset will be the end of his, and our, expeditions. I am curious to see what they do in Tamanrasset. No one I've corresponded with thinks there could be any oil there. The geology's all wrong.

"Mays is going to meet us in the room to bring us up to date. When I phoned him he said he's got a fist full of messages from the PM. Let's get some ice and a bottle of gin and go on upstairs. Our Mr. Mays likes his G and T."

Reggie mixes Terry Mays a gin and tonic, adds ice, and hands Mays the glass. "I take it things have been quiet in Ouargla while we've been gone?"

Mays raises his glass in salute before taking the first taste. "Oh I've had some excitement. That German Olaf has been making trouble. He came to the radio room looking for information about you two. He told me that Fairthorpe promised him she would cut him in on your gold treasure.

"He thinks Claire is trying to cut him out of his share of your gold. I told him to go to hell. I had to pull my pistol on him to keep him from killing me. The guy's a gorilla. He got drunk in the bar here and started beating up anyone he could get a hold of. Lom had to whack him on the head with a club to put him down.

"What did you make of our Mr. Bayers? From what contact I've had with him he seems a reasonable type. We had a good phone conversation; I think he will be a good man for the job. He is sending another man to help out here. The PM is of the opinion that the Jerrys are very interested in this part of Algeria."

Reggie finishes his beer. "I agree, Mays, he seems the right man for the job. But tell us what happened with Olaf?"

"Lom put him in his jail overnight and let him go the next day. The PM radioed me to give you the messages. His instruction was to decode them and type them up for you. He wants you to read them as he sent them without me embellishing. I must be off now. Thanks for the drink; I enjoyed it. Oh, and do watch out for Olaf."

Chapter 37

Professor Nast brings two bottles of Rhine wine with him for dinner. Reggie ordered mechoui, a roasted lamb dish served with the traditional couscous and mixed vegetables. No Algerian meal could be complete without a fresh French loaf to soak up the delicious juices.

Nast has the first wine bottle between his knees struggling with the corkscrew when the two waiters come in to set up the dining table. One man unfolds the table legs while the other man clears space for it. With practiced movements the table is set and the food is rolled in on a cart. The whole operation takes but minutes before Reggie and his guests sit at the table and the waiters leave.

As the heat of the day recedes, the ceiling fans bring the room to a comfortable temperature spreading rich aromas of roast lamb and fresh warm bread. Professor Nast reaches across the table to pour wine for Clive and Reggie. Setting the bottle down, he raises his glass, "A toast to friendship forged in a land of endless sands."

"That is quite poetic Professor," Reggie says. "This wine you brought will be excellent with the lamb. It's so crisp it makes me think of a cold mountain spring winding its way to the Rhine."

BOBO'S RAID

"Oh please Count, the thought of home tugs at my old heart. I wish this expedition was over. I long to feel those cool winds and to see the spring flowers blooming on the hillsides at home. I think this will be my last outing. Living in a tent with blowing sands, fierce flies covering the food, and for months on end is more than I can abide. I take solace that Tamanrasset will mark the end of this trip."

Reggie carves the lamb and places the plate in the middle of the table. "I'm sure after you've been home for a few months you'll be ready for another outing Professor."

"I'm not so sure Count. There is a lot of work to do at home. I will travel to some of the Grands Prix when work allows. Where do you go from here?"

"Clive and I are anxious to get back home also. We have to map the railroad route to Tamanrasset. That will wrap up our trip. We sold the Citroën to Marshal Balbo so that part of the enterprise has been successful."

Nast pushes his glasses up his nose to look into Reggie's face across the table. "Please be careful Count. Remember the Fairthorpe woman told us about your mission for Smyth. The Commander will be on the lookout for you. He does not want you to interfere with our mission. I have tried to persuade my people not to harm you. I do need to warn you the dummkopf Olaf is after you."

Clive passes a plate of vegetables to Nast. "How is Olaf after us? Isn't he with your people?"

"He was, but he has been trouble from the time we arrived here. Apparently his latest lunacy was to steal the money that was supposed to be for supplies. He is a drunkard and a bully. The men who were on the plane with us were to take him back to Germany to stand before a military court. He escaped from them and is on the loose. God only knows what more troubles he will bring. Fairthorpe convinced him you two had found the Mali gold. He thinks you are planning to get it out of the country."

"Claire Fairthorpe!" Reggie barks. "I am tired of the troubles that she-devil brings. Having her in the service of your country is the best thing your rivals could hope for."

"Steady on old man," Clive interjects.

Nast blinks. "You are not alone in that assessment. I fear she will be her own undoing."

"Sorry Professor," Reggie shrugs. "So how does your work go? Will that be a better subject? I know geology is the work you enjoy."

"Yes, geology is my interest, and, from what our Miss Claire says, your intelligence people are on to us. So I will tell you, I believe there is oil here."

Reggie stops eating, abruptly putting down his fork. "Please Professor, I do not want you to say anything that could harm you."

"I am just not the cloak and dagger type Count. However I am not being disloyal to my country. We live in a world that is by no means oil-poor. From a strictly economic standpoint the cost of producing oil from Algeria would be prohibitive. I do not think the French would be happy to have us here either."

"Then why go on to Tamanrasset Professor?"

"Well, my boy, it is because that is my instruction."

"The American oil men I contacted do not believe there is any oil to the south of here, sir."

"Do not be too clever Count. There are dangers that I can not protect you from."

"Does that mean you're really after something else?"

"We are officially here to dig for artifacts that will prove the German people were involved in the creation of civilization. I suggest we employ a different subject to continue to enjoy our dinner."

Nast is careful not to drink too much wine this night. The rest of the dinner conversation is of Clive and Reggie's racing adventures and the professor's humorous stories about blunders he and his colleagues made in the field.

Hours later, the Professor brings his hand over his mouth to cover another yawn. "This has been quite pleasant gentlemen but I believe it is well past my bedtime. Thank you for dinner."

Reggie turns his wrist to see his watch. "It is later than I thought. Dinner was our pleasure. I'll see you to your room."

Reggie shakes the Professor's hand at the door to his room. "Take care Professor. I hope we can meet again in Tamanrasset before you go home."

"Please Count, you should stay well clear of us in Tamanrasset. The commander has strict orders that you are not to interfere with our expedition. There are matters of science that must be well-guarded, as I am sure you can understand. I will reach you by radio to arrange a meeting if I can.

"You need to see that this is a serious business. You could be hurt or killed without me being able to prevent it. You are too much like your father I fear. Goodnight my boy."

Reggie, back in his room, calls the front desk to have the remains of the dinner removed. "I'll never make a great spy Jonesy. I was going to try to pump the Professor for more information but I couldn't do it. He was adamant about staying away from whatever they're doing in Tamanrasset. I need to radio London tomorrow. Maybe the PM can find out what would be valuable there.

"I'll see you in the morning. We need to see Captain Lom before we leave. I want to be on the road well before the Professor's trucks pull out."

Clive clicks his heels together snapping his arm to a salute. "Rightyo, old drill master. Knock me up in the morning will you?"

Chapter 38

Reggie calls Clive's room to wake him late the next morning.

"Rise and shine, m'lad. I'm hungry. Let's get some breakfast."

Clive and Reggie, seated by large open windows, enjoy the cool fresh morning air. The restaurant smells of strong coffee and spicy vegetables. Before they place an order Captain Lom sits down at their table with a cup of steaming coffee in hand.

"Bonjour mes amis. How did you go in Tripoli?"

Reggie grins. "Good morning to you Lom, it's good to see you. We go very well Captain, please join us for breakfast. How does everything go for you? I understand you've had some excitement."

"Oui, the excitement here seems to come with the two of you. We have the spies and now the ill-tempered Boche. This German, Olaf, is a bad one. It is the two of you he is after. I had him in my jail for a night but could not keep him. He paid for the damage he made here, that was all I could do. Now two German police want him too. They are mad that I do not hold him, but he is gone like the smoke.

"But for me I am happy he is gone. The man cried all night in the cell, pouring out his life's story to the poor unfortunate in the next cell. He bitterly complained of a father who beat him and a mother who did not love him. His schoolmates thought him dumb. He said he left school early and found salvation in the Nazi party.

"The Nazis put him with others like him. They roamed the streets beating up anyone who would not return their Nazi salutes. This Olaf boasted that the Nazis promoted him because he became the strongest of his gang of bullies."

Reggie sets his coffee down frowning. "Where do you think the man went?"

"I can not be sure," Lom replies. "He has money, quite a sum the German police say. With money he could buy transportation anywhere. I have sent out the bulletins but this is an easy country to be lost. Perhaps if he finds trouble to send him to a lockup we will get him."

"So why do you think he is looking for us?" Clive asks.

Lom's face lights up in a smile. "It is for the gold you are trying smuggle out of my country. From the big noises he makes here, he will not be the only one after this gold."

Reggie shakes his head. "You know we don't have any gold, Lom."

Lom bites into a croissant sending a cascade of crumbs down the napkin tucked into his tunic. After some chewing he says, "It is my understanding that you are men of great wealth and have no need of more money. I have learned however that some men can never have enough."

Reggie pulls his coffee close as the waiter brings breakfast. "We did not come for gold and we will soon be out of your hair. After stocking up the Citroën, we'll be leaving for Tamanrasset. I doubt we'll see you again my friend. The Citroën is sold to Marshal Balbo so we've planned to fly home from Tamanrasset."

Lom shrugs. "I was, what you English say, giving you the mickey, or is it taking from you the mickey? I will be sorry to see you go. I have grown to covet your brandy. It is a long way to Fort Laperrine. This, of course, is the proper French name for what you are saying is Tamanrasset. No matter what route you take, it is a long and hard journey. There are many dangers; you will be far from the safety of our forts until you arrive in Fort Laperrine."

Clive wipes a napkin across his mouth. "We are well-armed, well-provisioned, and well-protected in our truck. Marauding bandits should be very wary of trying to attack us. They're only reward will be a great deal of well-aimed lead."

Lom, taken aback by Clive's vehemence, shrugs. "Please check in with me when you are ready to leave. If you have some idea of when you will reach Fort Laperrine I will advise them."

Lom pushes back from the table and, rising, squares his cap. "Take care mes amis."

Reggie and Clive rise to shake hands with the captain. "Thank you for your help," Reggie says. "It has been our pleasure to meet you. We'll check in before we leave, and I'll radio here to let you know how we are getting on."

Sitting back down after the captain leaves, Reggie turns to Clive. "Well, Jonesy, we can't say we haven't been warned. Let's finish breakfast and get the truck ready. I think it will be a good idea to stop on the outskirts of town and give a demonstration of our firepower. I'll tell Mays and Lom to spread the word."

Standing at the back of the Citroën, Reggie checks off the items on his list. Clive, on a blanket beneath the truck, pumps the handle of a grease gun. He carefully wipes away any residual grease so as not to attract sand.

Clive crawls out from under the truck. "That's the last of the maintenance done. What's next?"

"We just need to get enough dates to fill the grain sacks that will be our bandit targets."

Reggie and Clive emerge from the souq, or marketplace, with four old sacks of dates and one smaller sack of tomatoes. Bartering with a vender over buying the old Arab robes took most the time. A young boy pushes the wheeled cart they hired some half a kilometer to the Citroën.

After loading the last sack in the back of the Citroën, Reggie gets behind the steering wheel. "We've got a couple of hours before our demo. We'll get some lunch on the way."

Just outside a break in the date palms on the outside of town, Reggie steps back to inspect the two figures Clive is working on. "Looks good Jonesy; we've already attracted a gathering. As soon as Lom shows up we'll get the show going."

The two ersatz Arab bandits stand in front of a small dune. A bit of a breeze tugs at the robes. Captain Lom talks to Reggie who stands by the Citroën parked twenty yards from the date and tomato-filled figures. "I spread the words that you would show the teeth of your Citroën. As one can see you have a good audience."

Reggie shakes Lom's hand. "Thanks again. We'll be off after the show."

BOBO'S RAID

Inside the Citroën Clive opens the shutter and rests his Thompson machine gun on the ledge. "I'm ready old gangster."

"Okay Jonesy, fire one 30-clip into the one on your right. I'll fire my clip into the one on the left just as you stop. Then you jump out the back and pitch your grenade. Jump back in and we'll tear off."

Clive opens up on the figure. Bullets rip into the robes shredding the tomatoes placed in front of the dates that make up the bulk of the figures. The torn robes run with scarlet. Reggie opens up on the other figure as if it is one murderous volley. Pieces of robe fly off as the figure's ruined red-stained mess topples to the ground.

Clive shoves the rear doors open, steps out and throws the grenade. A huge cloud of sand flies up as the figures disappear. The noise and concussion of the explosion scatter some of the crowd while others duck to the ground.

Reggie starts the truck and waits for Clive to get in. The Citroën throws up twin rooster tails of sand off the tracks as it disappears around a stand of date palms.

Chapter 39

Reggie pumps the camp stove to life under the coffee pot. The rising sun has the Citroën casting a long shadow. Clive and Reggie are camped high on a flat-topped hill overlooking the southern side of the city. Clive walks toward his campstool yawning while scratching his backside. "Morning old early bird, any sign of the worm?"

"I haven't seen any trucks stir on my watch. I think the professor's group must be late risers."

Clive rubs his hands over the camp stove. "Are we going to follow them all the way to Tamanrasset?"

Reggie adds coffee to the boiling water. "No, we have the day they told Lom they would be at Fort Laperrine. That doesn't give them any time to take a side trip. I believe whatever they're after is in, or fairly close around, Tamanrasset. Keep low and the sun at your back while you watch for 'em. I'm going to get a little sleep."

Clive shakes Reggie awake. "Wakie wakie, the trucks are pulling out."

"Stay low," Clive warns. "The commander already stopped the lead truck once and scanned the area with his binoculars."

Reggie lies on his belly and brings his binoculars up to his eyes.

BOBO'S RAID

"They're headed west Jonesy. That'll take them to In Salah, then southeast to Tamanrasset. I told the professor that we'd head east then south to map the railroad route. I'm sure the commander figures if he sees us on his route that we're on their trail for sure. I don't know if he'd try to confront us or just evade us. It's going to be hard to find out what they're up to without them being wise to us."

Clive backs away. "Shall I get the Citroën warmed up, old scout?"

"Hold up a bit Jonesy. I want to watch till they're out of sight."

Clive settles by Reggie. Both men, binoculars up to their eyes, watch as the two German trucks accompanied by clouds of dust become smaller in the distance. Now miles away the dust clouds diminish as the haze on the horizon makes the images they see with their binoculars shimmer. A brilliant flash of light sparks their attention.

"What was that?" Clive exclaims.

Reggie fingers the knob to adjust the focus. "It's the sun reflecting off the commander's binoculars. They've stopped again. I can just make him out. Schulz must really be anxious."

Clive and Reggie watch as the trucks fade over the horizon. Reggie gets up and dusts the front of his shirt and pants off. "Might as well get the camp gear loaded up Jonesy."

"Are we going to saddle up?" Clive asks.

"We don't have to be in any great hurry. We'll be able to cover a lot more ground in a day than they can. Our best bet to find what the professor is really after is to get to Tamanrasset a couple of days before they do.

We can reconnoiter the area and radio London to see if they have any ideas."

Finishing the last of the coffee, they secure the camp gear in the back of the Citroën. As Reggie steps up to the cab of the truck he sees a cloud of dust from a car leaving the city. He grabs his binoculars and walks back to the edge of the hill to get a better look.

Clive comes around the truck to see what is happening. "What do you see old eagle eye?"

Reggie hands the binoculars to Clive. "It's an old open top Fiat 503. See if you can make out who's driving."

Clive looks though the binoculars, fidgets with the focus knob before looking at Reggie incredulously. "I'll be damned. It's Claire Fairthorpe. Where the hell is she going?"

Reggie takes the binoculars from Clive. "Let's watch and see."

Clive runs back to the truck for his binoculars. The two men watch as the old Fiat races across the flat ground below them. Bucking like a wild bronco over the uneven trail, the car follows the tracks made by the German trucks. Eventually the car travels out of their sight.

Clive lowers his binoculars. "She must be chasing the Germans."

Reggie turns toward the Citroën. "Maybe that's what Schulz was watching for. The woman will fry her head in this sun; she must be in a hurry."

"Her brain's already fried," Clive exclaims.

The trip from Ouargla to Tamanrasset is over 550 miles. The men take turns driving during the day and keeping watch at night. The trail consists of coarse stone pebbles along the flats, then sand dunes that lead into a wadi or an ancient river bed, some that have been dry for centuries. The wadis snake between mountains and foothills.

On the third day Clive is driving his shift. Coming around a bend he stops the Citroën. Reggie's head snaps up from his nap. "What's up Jonesy?"

"Looks like a rock slide ahead Reg. I think we can drive over it if we clear a few of the bigger rocks on top. We're in a blind canyon the walls are too steep to drive up. I can back up. There's not enough room to turn around."

Reggie opens the door to the Citroën to climb out. "Hold on, I'll take a look." He jumps back in and slams the door shut. "Get in the back and break out the Thompson's. We've got bandits all around us."

The roof of the Citroën blocks Clive's view so he can't see the bandits on the top of the walls and thinks of backing up the Citroën. One look in the door's rear view mirror sends him scurrying though the opening in the cab to the rear compartment. He yells to Reggie over his shoulder. "They're coming up behind us on horseback!"

He hands Reggie a Thompson submachine gun through the opening. "Stay in the back Jonesy. Hold your fire. Let's see if they want to talk first."

Clive goes to the rear of the Citroën and opens a gun port in one of the windowless rear doors. He sticks the short barrel of his Thompson through the port and almost instantly receives a volley of gunfire from the horsemen. Reggie scrambles through from the front bulkhead to Clive's side. Sporadic gunfire comes from the horsemen; bullets make a dull metallic thud off the armor plated doors.

"I don't want one of those guys sending a wild shot into our fuel jugs on top." Reggie opens the gun port on the side of the Citroën and aims up the side of the canyon wall before him. "Fire a volley at the horses' feet; we don't want to kill the riders if we don't have to."

Both men open fire. 45-caliber bullets from the Thompson's tear into the dirt inches away from the horses. The horses rear up, their riders fighting to stay in the saddles. One of the riders on the canyon wall above Reggie, pitches over the head of his horse and down the canyon wall. The man hits the ground hard with his arms stretched out in front of him. The deafening gunfire stops. The only noise is the horses snorting and stomping the ground.

Reggie goes to the front of the Citroën to see about the man who fell. The man lies close the passenger side door of the truck, his right arm lies bent at an odd angle to his body. The man rises to his knees, his dark face turning pale with pain. Reggie whips open the door, quickly grabbing the man to pull him inside the Citroën.

Reggie topples into the Citroën on his back with the Berber on top of him. He hooks the door latch with his foot and pulls the door closed. Reggie squirms out from under the man. He tries to be as gentle as possible tugging the semi-conscious man down to the floor between the seats. The Berber groans as his broken arm contacts the floor.

"What's going on?" Clive yells.

"It's okay; I pulled in a Berber that got thrown from his horse. I don't think the others are going to be shooting at us with their man in here. At least I hope they don't. If you think it's safe to leave your gun port I need to splint this man's arm broken arm. I'll need you to cut me a couple of pieces of a shovel handle about two feet long."

Reggie works to get the Berber's robes off to treat the broken arm. He pulls the Berber's turban from his head to use as a pillow. As he straightens the Berber's broken arm the man comes to. There is fire in his eyes; he goes for Reggie's throat with his good arm. Reggie straddles the Berber's chest with his knee on the man's good arm.

Clive comes through the opening in the bulkhead with two pieces of shovel handle. "Do you need help with him, Reg? What's he saying?"

"I'm not sure. I think it's some brand of French and if that's it, he's telling me to go ahead and kill him."

Reggie, in his own brand of French, tries, with a calm low voice, to assure the Berber that he does not want to kill him. He tells the man, and at the same time pantomimes with his hands, that they are trying to fix his broken arm.

"What's he on about now, Reg?"

"I think he wants to know why we'd help him."

Clive puts down the handle parts next to the Berber. "Well tell the silly sod it's just like when we dug the bloody well for his mates up north."

Reggie looks up at Clive. "That's an excellent idea. Who said you were just a pretty face?"

"Sod off," Clive says with a smile.

A different light comes into the Berber's eyes as he begins to comprehend Reggie's broken French and hand gestures. Together Clive and Reggie bind the wood splints to his arm. Then they help him to sit up and Clive brings water for him to drink. The outside has been quiet for some time. Clive goes to the back to see what the horsemen behind them are up to.

The men are talking amongst themselves standing beside their horses. One of the Berbers slides down the canyon wall to stand in front of the Citroën. He stands on the pile of rocks to see inside the truck. Raising his arm he calls to the Berber in the Citroën. The Berber in the Citroën raises his good arm and calls back to the man.

Clive returns to the front. "What are they on about old doctor?"

"I think the man we have here may be the leader. I hope he's telling the other he's okay."

More of the Berbers gather in front of the Citroën and begin to pull the rocks away.

Clive takes a long drink of water. "I say, my old hero, that looks positive."

Reggie and the Berber talk back and forth until they begin to understand each other. Clive watches the two men: the Berber with only one arm to communicate with is finding that difficult.

Reggie turns to Clive. "I think got I've the gist of it. He is thanking us for taking care of him and he has heard about our well-digging. He wants us to come to their camp and have dinner or something like that."

Clive caps his canteen. "Can we just be on our way? I'm not sure I want to be in the middle of an armed camp. Anyway if we want to get ahead of the Jerrys we should be going, don't you think?"

Reggie goes back to speaking to the Berber. "Help me get him to his feet and pull his clothes back on. He says he understands and that we won't have any problem with bandits in this region."

Outside of the Citroën the Berbers gather around the broken- armed leader. He speaks to his tribesmen, then turns to Reggie to thank him. He takes a curved knife in a jeweled scabbard from his belt to give to Reggie. Reggie steps forward to take the knife and extends his hand to shake hands.

Clive opens the door to the Citroën. "Lets get the bloody blue blazes out of here, old Stanley."

Chapter 40

On the fifth day of their travels they enter the Hoggar Mountains. Fort Laperrine, as the French have named the city, commands the center of the city. It lies some 4300 feet above sea level.

The Citroën jounces over the rough terrain going up the mountain trail. Reggie looks over at Clive's dust-covered face. "I know you're ready to sink in a tub of cool water, but I don't want the fort's commander to know we're here yet. Can you hang on for a day or two?"

Clive spits out of his window. "I've eaten enough sand, old slaver, but I take your point. We've the portable shower and enough water now that we're here, so as long as I'm the first one in, we're good."

Reggie laughs. "When I saw your face covered with dust, I thought you'd be a bit put out."

"Yours is no improvement," Clive warns. "You're no Rudolf Valentino."

Reggie glances at himself in the side mirror. "I meant you looked like you were thinking of a cold drink and a good meal."

Clive blows the grit from his nose in his handkerchief. "I was actually thinking we sold this old girl too cheap. We go five days without a glimmer of problem. She just glides over ground that would kill any other vehicle. I know it was a ruse to get here but

I've grown fond of this little beastie. I won't mind building and selling more of these when we get home."

"Good on you Jonesy; if Marshal Balbo likes this one, we may be up to our eyeballs in orders. What we have to concentrate on now is what the Germans are after."

Clive points forward. "Lead on McDuff."

Chapter 41

Many miles behind Clive and Reggie, Olaf Fischer's hands bled. Frustrated trying to follow the Citroën through the desert he hammered the steering wheel of the old model A Ford he had bought. The hard material of the steering wheel rim cracked apart under the fierce pounding of his fist. Each time the old car bounced over a rut or stones on the trail, the steering wheel kicked back, ripping at the flesh on his palms.

Following the Citroën the previous day, Fischer kept watch through the night. Realizing almost too late that the men in the Citroën were going to camp out on top of the hill, he found a place to hide while keeping a vigil. The Citroën clattered down the hill and struck out across the rough trail east.

Keeping enough distance not to be noticed, Olaf keeps pace. The morning's cool air soon turns warm. Before long, the Citroën gets smaller in the distance. When the Citroën turns south Olaf almost loses it. Pebbles clack up under the fenders, the Ford leaps from one rut to another beating the driver mercilessly. Only an ever-diminishing cloud of dust hanging in the air marks the trail of the Citroën.

Sweating hard now, Olaf tries to speed up. The Ford shakes violently, beating itself to death on the rough trail. The cloud of dust is gone, only clumps of rock and scrub shimmer in the heat for as far as he can see.

Olaf stops the car as plumes of steam billow from the radiator. High noon heat beats down. Ripping strips of cloth from a shirt, he wraps the cloth around his palms as a bandage. After adding water to the hissing radiator, he sits in the car to sip some of the water. Sitting with his head in his hands, he realizes he cannot follow the Citroën. The grand plan to trail Reggie and Clive to the gold is a failure. Close to despair, Olaf is not sure if he can even find his way back to Ouargla.

The torn fabric of the cloth top does little to shelter Olaf from the punishing sun. Headed back north toward Ouargla, going slowly, trying to follow his tracks, he has plenty of time to think. Stealing the supply money, he now realizes, ruined him with the expedition and the Nazi party. The party leaders who trusted him to watch the expedition would want his blood.

It was the first time anyone trusted him with so much money. Now he could not return to the protection of the Nazi party. He had to find the gold Bobrowski was trying to get out of Algeria. "Those fools should have known I would take the money," he screams to the empty desert. "I will find some way to get them all! I'll get Claire Fairthorpe too. The source of all my troubles lies with that she-devil. She wants the gold to herself. Well, she'll pay. All of my enemies will be in Tamanrasset, I must get there."

Chapter 42

Traveling to the west out of the view of Fort Laperrine's tall tower, Reggie heads for the area of ore mining. A little over an hour later they see stark hillsides where open pit mining has carved huge gashes into the land. Farther on is a small village in a valley with little vegetation.

Both men are out of the Citroën stretching, arms in the air, backs arched. Children of the village gather timidly around the truck. One boy moves forward to touch the caterpillar track. Reggie opens the cab's door and motions for the boy to look inside. The boy goes to the door to peer inside. The other children run their hands over the tracks and join the boy at the door.

Reggie has his hand on the first boy's tunic to keep him from climbing inside the Citroën. The children are talking excitedly amongst themselves, their voices growing louder. Two women in black Berber robes come into the alley to see what the children are doing. Reggie asks the women in his halting French if there is a place to get a drink.

The women cock their heads trying to understand this strange language. Reggie brings his free hand to his mouth as if holding a glass. The boy whose tunic Reggie has in his hand, turns away from the door and tugs at Reggie's sleeve pointing down the narrow dusty alley.

"Jonesy, watch these little rascals will you? I'll go with this boy and see what he's pointing to."

"Will do, oh faithful leader. Don't get into any trouble will you."

The boy leads Reggie down the rough uneven lane. There are several one-story mud brick buildings on both sides of the alleyway. The buildings are a faded red color with flat roofs. At the end of the alley the boy pushes open a weathered, dark wood door. The boy stands to the side and points inside.

Reggie looks into the darkness of the room. He enters as his eyes begin to adjust to the darkness. Some light emanates from around wood shutters closed against window shaped openings in the far wall. The temperature of the small room is quite a bit cooler than outside. A man in Berber robes rises from a chair. The boy, who has pushed by Reggie, speaks to the Berber in a rapid tongue.

The man hustles the boy out of the room and motions Reggie to sit in a chair by a small table. Reggie sits as the man goes about making tea in a corner of the room. Pouring tea into a glass the man sets the glass on the table and goes back to his chair to sit. Reggie tastes the sweet tea and smiles to show his delight to the man in the chair.

As he sips the tea, Reggie is startled by the door being flung open. He turns to see the boy who brought him to the room leading a tall man in Berber robes. A headdress covers the man's face, leaving cold black eyes to stare out at Reggie.

Stepping to Reggie's table, the man flings out his arm. His hand, devoid of weapons, is extended. "Français?"

Recovering quickly Reggie shakes the man's hand. "I am English, Reggie Bobrowski, and you are?"

Unwrapping his headdress to reveal the wide pointed-tips mustache of an unmistakably French man, he says, "Forgive me for bursting in, Monsieur. When the boy said a man like me was in the village I rushed to see for myself. I am Claude de Long, the mining company's traveling physician. Pleased as I am to see another white man, what on earth brings you here?"

Reggie motions the man to sit. "My partner and I are here field-testing our Citroën and mapping a railroad route. Tamanrasset is the end of our journey. I am very interested in what sort of industries are here."

The doctor speaks to the man in Berber asking for tea. He then turns his attention to Reggie. "I thought the Trans-Saharan railroad was a folly. Do you really think it is possible?"

"It could be," Reggie replies. "We are trying to see if there is enough trade to support such a project. What do you think of the possibility? We could certainly use an informed view, but first I would like to go get my partner. He's guarding the Citroën."

"Of course," the doctor says. "I'll have the boy here look after your Citroën. No one will trouble it to be sure."

Reggie and Clive return to the tea room. "Doctor De Long, this is my friend, Clive Parry-Jones. Jonesy meet Doctor De Long."

After shaking hands Clive sits at the table. "Pleased to meet you doctor. Do you look after the mining business here?"

"In some respects. My main job is to look after the men who work the mines."

Clive takes a long drink from the glass of tea he is served. "Thank you, that is refreshing. What sort of mining goes on here doctor?"

"The area is rich in uranium," De Long answers.

"Uranium?" Reggie asks. "I'm really not familiar with it. What is it used for?"

"The largest use," the doctor explains, "is in coloring glass and pottery glazes. Radium is a by product that is used for glow-in-the-dark clock dials. It takes many tons of uranium to make a gram of radium. So the uranium waste is an inexpensive commodity to sell to the glass and pottery industry.

"The price of radium is very high. I read that many doctors in Europe and America are still making claims that radium will cure everything from cancer to sicknesses of the heart."

"How do you transport the ore to market?" Reggie asks.

"By trucks now," the doctor replies. "If there were a train I am sure it would be used to take the material to port. However the train has been proposed and argued about for many years. No one can agree who will pay to build it, or by what route it would run."

Clive's face clouds with a question. "I've been trying to think of what was it I read about radium. Oh, by jove, isn't it deadly?"

"It is if ingested," De Long replies. "I do not believe there is enough evidence of what happens with long term external exposure."

"Are there any ill effects to exposure to uranium?" Reggie asks.

"I don't believe the ore itself is harmful, however I am finding that men who work in the underground mines suffer from respiratory aliments, or lung cancers. I believe the cause is the dust or a gas emitted in an unventilated space. Are you two interested in uranium mining yourselves? We seem to have had quite a bit of interest since the Italians, and Germans began to publish their work."

Clive and Reggie trade looks. Reggie leans forward on the table. "What works are you speaking of doctor?"

"I'm afraid that is somewhat beyond my scope gentlemen. The Italians apparently bombarded uranium with something that produced two new atomic elements. I think that is what I read. The Germans have some more secretive work they are doing. I have a group on the way here that is going to do their own mining. My company is very curious. I am to offer every assistance."

"Do your travels take you to Tamanrasset, doctor?"

"Fort Laperrine please," De Long cautions. "We are a French country gentlemen. Oui, my duties take me there often. I send my reports to my company from there."

Reggie finishes his tea. "We would be very pleased if we could invite you to dinner in Fort Laperrine doctor. I believe we have much to learn from you in regards to a potential railroad."

"It would be my pleasure gentlemen. When would it be convenient? My next report is due in two days. Where will you be staying?"

"We will be at the Hotel du Hoggar. Is the food good there?"

"Mais oui, most excellent. I will look forward to dining with you."

BOBO'S RAID

Reggie stands and extends his hand to De Long. "We have a lot to do before we get to Fort Laperrine doctor, please excuse us. This has been a very fortunate meeting. We appreciate your help. Dinner, I'm sure, will be a pleasure."

Reggie puts a coin on the table. Clive shakes the doctor's hand before the men leave the little tea room.

Turning the Citroën back toward Tamanrasset, Reggie laughs. "By god, I can't believe the luck. We need to find some high ground and radio London. We've done it Jonesy!"

Pulling off his headphones after signing off, Reggie begins decoding the answer from London. Thumbing to the page in his codebook for today's message, he busies the pencil. The Citroën rocks as Clive climbs in the back door. "Well, old Morse, can we go home now?"

"Sorry Jonesy, London wants us to stay until we're sure what the Germans are up to. I thought we were on our way home too. They're right though. We aren't sure if it's the professor's group that is coming to do the mining. We shouldn't have to wait long to find out."

Chapter 43

Ten miles outside of Ouargla, Olaf's Ford trails a thin black line of oil as it bounces over the rough terrain. With Ouargla in sight, the old car's engine begins to rattle.

Olaf's anger grows as the engine loses power; he jams his foot down on the throttle. The engine, with no oil left to lubricate it, seizes, locking up the rear wheels, kicking up a cloud of dust. Olaf, teeth bared, throws the door open, then jumps out to kick the fender viciously.

The leaking oil finds metal hot enough to ignite it. Consumed by rage Olaf bangs his fist down on the hood. Flames leap from the hood's louvers. In an instant, the front of the car burns furiously.

Stumbling back to land on his butt, he jumps up to pull his bags out of the car. A pall of smoke rises from behind him as he trudges toward Ouargla. With the heavy bags pulling at his tortured hands, the town seems much farther away.

Chapter 44

Having sent the radio message, Reggie drives the Citroën down the steep decline to return to the valley below. A rain of shale, pebbles, and sand follow the truck. Skidding on the loose surface at a sharp turn of the goat trail, Clive looks out of his side to see the trail disappear. "I say, old shepherd, you know there's nothing under this old girl. It's hundreds of feet to the valley floor."

Just as the Citroën slides toward another ledge, Reggie fights the steering wheel. While his hands are busy making quick corrections at the wheel, he grins at Clive. "It's okay Jonesy, we don't have much farther to go before there's better ground."

Clive rolls his eyes, and, although not Catholic, elaborately crosses himself.

The trail opens up and Reggie stops to take in the panoramic view of Tamanrasset. Bringing up his binoculars he scans the valley and Fort Laperrine.

"This place reminds me of the American southwest. Americans call these kinds of flat-topped mountains mesas. The red rust-colors of the land and mountain-sides look the same too."

Clive wipes sweat from his forehead. "Can we go get a bath and a good meal now, oh mighty pathfinder? You've failed to kill us once more; I'd like to bathe just to prove I'm still with the living."

"But, of course, my melodramatic friend; let's go see what fabulous delights await at Fort Laperrine."

Fort Laperrine dominates the small city that has grown around it. The fort is a large sprawling structure, with high crenelated walls. The faded red walls completely enclose many buildings inside. There are trees, parade grounds, stables, garages, barracks, and a high metal tower that rises a hundred feet above the walls.

The red clay, that is so prominent in the terrain, is used for making bricks. These bricks make up the small flat-topped buildings that line the dusty streets. In contrast to the red colors, the Tuareg men busy the streets in their dark blue robes. Trees, with white painted trunks, dot the landscape providing a welcome shade.

Entering the city, the Citroën soon draws the curious. When Reggie stops at the hotel a small crowd gathers to touch the caterpillar's tracks. A small round-bellied Frenchman comes out of the hotel to welcome the travelers and shoo away the crowd.

"Welcome gentlemens. I am manager here. We have you the rooms. You may be pleased to put your Citroën in the rear."

The hotel, not as large or continental as the one in Ouargla, has comfortable rooms and baths. The red brick walls are three feet thick to keep out the brutal heat of the summer. A small courtyard, with gravel paths winding through trees and scrubs, is nestled behind the hotel.

After bathing Clive knocks on Reggie's door. "Are you awake old stick? I'm hungry enough to eat the backside of a camel."

Reggie, wiping shaving cream from his face, opens his door.

"Camels rump I'm sure is on the menu. Hang on while I get a shirt on and we'll see what we can find."

The restaurant in the hotel is small but the food is very good. Both men order a lamb dish with a nice French wine.

Clive pours more wine into his glass. "What's up for the morrow Reg?"

"We can sleep in. Sometime tomorrow we should check in with the commandant at the Fort. Lom said he would have the commandant be on the lookout for us. I'll take him a bottle of the brandy Lom likes so much. It can't hurt to be in his good graces. I want to scout around to get familiar with the area. With all of the mountains around here we should find a good vantage point to observe the Germans at work when they get here."

"I hope," Clive says with some concern in voice, "that you can find a mountain with a better trail than the one today."

"We'll drive to the west and see what we can find. We may need to camp out to be able to find out what our quarry's up to. You can drive if you'd like."

Clive sits his wine glass down. "No thanks, old goater, I'd rather keep my eyes closed."

Chapter 45

Having found his way to Ouargla, Olaf Fischer, disguised in Arab garb, boards the tour bus bound for Fort Laperrine. The seats at the front of the bus are already occupied. Settling in a seat he soon becomes aware that the bus carries more than tourists. Old Berber men, along with their goats and sheep come aboard. Berber women bring their small children.

Olaf is never far from being in a foul mood. Children crying and goats trying to chew his bootlaces push his anger to the limit. He lashes out at the goat and screams at the women whose children are crying. The bus driver stops the bus and walks back to stand over Olaf.

Before the driver can get a word out, Olaf pushes back the hood that hid his face, then stands and grabs the driver's shirt to drag him to the front of the bus. He shoves the driver down behind the bus's giant steering wheel. "Drive you miserable bastard!" Olaf screams. The driver, not withstanding the fact that he is French and does not understand German, does get the message.

Olaf turns to glower at the rest of the bus' occupants before walking back to his seat. Once the bus is underway dust and sand fill the bus. Most of the dust and grit collects toward the back of the bus. Olaf stands grabbing the seat backs going forward to keep his balance as the bus jostles over the rough road. At the front of the bus, he pulls a tourist from his seat behind the driver.

Pointing toward the back of the bus with his thumb, Olaf sends the tourist packing. The woman in the same seat grabs her bags and follows. Olaf sits sideways in the seat to watch the passengers as well as ahead. The driver glances up in the big rear view mirror above the windshield but does not meet Olaf's angry gaze. He quickly brings his eyes back to the road ahead.

The bus stops several times to let people off and pick up others. The driver climbs to the top of the bus to retrieve luggage and gas cans to replenish the bus' gas tank. They drive through the night at a much slower pace. While stopped for fuel the driver makes coffee on a camp stove. He drinks several cups, relieves himself behind some bushes, then drives on.

The next day goes on much the same. At the end of the day, they stop at a small town. The driver announces that they will stop here for the night. There is a small restaurant and a few guest rooms in the back of a shabby clay house. Olaf pushes past to be the first to get a room and a meal. With Olaf gone, the bus driver speaks in low tones to the remaining passengers before they go into their rooms for the night.

When Olaf wakes the next morning, the sun is high. He swings his legs out of the bed and goes down the deserted hallway to the toilet. It is not until he returns to his room that he notices the lack of any activity. Throwing on his shirt, he dashes through the place and out the front to find an empty lot. The bus and the passengers have gone. Cursing with rage, he stomps into the restaurant.

Chapter 46

Claire Fairthorpe was still angry. Her Nazi master ordered her to take a new type of Geiger counter to the professor's expedition. She knew this was a punishment for her failures with Bobrowski and her subordinates in Ouargla. Moreover, not only was she a wanted criminal in Algeria, she had to find her own transportation to get the professor his new equipment.

An old Fiat was all she could find in a hurry. She was already a day behind the time she was to meet the expedition. She had almost caught up with the trucks when, just outside Ouargla, the Fiat's right front tire exploded in a rut. She watched the dust cloud made by the expedition's trucks fade in the distance. Claire worked the rest of the day getting the spare tire on. She spent the night alone in the freezing desert trying to sleep.

It took two more days of hard driving to catch up to the German trucks. She handed off the Geiger counter to the professor before she turned back on the road to get out of Algeria. She planned to go north until she could find the road that led to the west where she could get out of Algeria and into Morocco.

She hated the desert, the heat, and the sand. Going north, she fell asleep and ran off the road into a ravine. A rear tire punctured on a sharp rock with a bang that jolted her awake. The useless tire slipped on the rim as she rocked the car back and forth to get back on the road. By the time she got to the small town, the tire and wheel were ruined.

It took two more days until a bus brought a new wheel and tire from Ouargla. The morning was still cold when the Berber finished putting the new wheel and tire on her Fiat. She paid the man and drove around the front of the restaurant to buy water and gas. She was putting the water away when her head snapped back. Someone had a fistful of her hair.

"Well, well, look who's here to drive me to Fort Laperrine." Olaf's fetid breath strikes her nostrils at same time she recognizes his voice.

Claire puts her hand to her hair trying to twist out of Olaf's grasp. "What the hell are you doing here? Let go of my hair!"

The women in the little restaurant shrink back when Olaf drags Claire with him to pick up his bags at the door. Claire shouts in a guttural language they do not understand. Olaf puts down his bags and slaps her hard. Claire's tries to clear her head as he drags her back to the car.

Claire fights Olaf clawing at his face, her finger nails drawing blood. Olaf punches her hard on her jaw. Claire goes limp, he roughly dumps her into the car before driving south. Claire wakes to find her clothes torn.

"God damn you! I'll kill you Olaf."

"No, it is I who will kill you, witch. You will tell me where Bobrowski has the gold or I will kill you very slowly."

"Gold! You idiot there is no gold. That was just a story to get you to do your job."

Olaf stops the car, then turns and slaps her face. "You better hope you can get me that gold. I would enjoy destroying you a little at a time."

Claire tries to vault over the car's door. Olaf grabs her hair then turns her face toward him to punch her. When Claire comes to, her arms and legs are tied with strips of her clothing.

Chapter 47

Reggie and Clive enter the Fort Laperrine commandant's office to find that he does not speak English. The man is slender, his face lined and dark from the sun. Rising from his desk, his posture is stiff which makes him seem somewhat aloof. He shakes their hands with the proper firmness. The officer who translates does so in such a halting manner Reggie and Clive keep their conversation as short as possible.

When Reggie presents the commandant with the bottle of brandy, a brilliant smile flashes across his face. Pulling the pince-nez glasses from his nose, the commandant focuses them over the bottle's label. Stepping around his desk, he enthusiastically shakes Reggie's hand again, then turns to Clive to shake his hand. Speaking to his officer, he motions to Reggie and Clive.

The officer nods to the commandant. "My captain would like to say his happiness. He is saying to come to him when you have some need. Comprenez-vous?"

Out of the cool air of the commandant's office, the fierce sun heats the desert. Clive pulls off his jacket to sling it over his shoulder. The winter's cooler days are gone now. "Mercy, it's an oven out here already."

Reggie climbs behind the steering wheel of the Citroën, waiting for Clive to settle in. "We need to scout the territory; let's get that done first. When we find good locations to observe from, we can head back to the hotel to mark our maps and have a cool drink. I'm hoping dinner with Doctor De Long will answer a lot of questions for us."

That evening Doctor De Long is sitting in the hotel's restaurant sipping a glass of red wine when Reggie and Clive arrive. "Good evening gentlemen, I have been looking forward to a good dinner. Shall we take a table?"

Reggie reaches out to shake the Doctor's hand. "Yes indeed. Very good of you to join us Doctor. How are things at the mines?"

De Long takes a seat at one of the eight small tables in the restaurant. "I think quite exciting things are happening. I have just come from making my report which I do from the radio at the fort. The Germans came in today and I showed them our richest mine. The professor has the latest Geiger counter which is much smaller in size than anything I've seen.

"The professor took counts from the mine and our ore samples. He has offered to buy our entire company. I can tell you he is offering quite a goodly sum. There are no particulars as yet so I cannot say what my company may do. However I did speak with the professor about upgrading my medical facilities. He thought that would be in line with what his company would want also.

"I could do some studies on the gases emitted and I hope we can make a better life for the miners and their families. These men work hard and get very little in return. When the bread winner falls ill, his family is in ruin. So I have good hope for the future."

"I hate to put a damper on, old man, but…"

"Hold on Clive," Reggie interjects. "Our experience with the Jerrys doesn't mean the professor's group will be like that."

"What do you speak of, gentlemen?" the doctor asks.

Reggie answers quickly. "The Germans are not… let me say, the most compassionate of men. However the professor is a man of integrity."

"You know him, the professor?" De Long asks.

"Yes, I do," Reggie answers. "He and my father were great friends."

"How marvelous," De Long exclaims. "He has just entered the restaurant."

Reggie turns in his chair to see Nast walk in. "Professor, it is so good to see you."

Nast moves to the table and, as Reggie rises from his chair, Nast forgoes a handshake and hugs Reggie. "Forgive the non-German hug, my son, but it is good to see you too. I do so hate this desert. It is a pleasure to see a friend.

"Doctor, you know Reggie and Clive I see. What a wonderful surprise. May we dine together?"

De Long stands from his seat. "These gentlemen invited me to dinner sir. I did not know you were friends. I would most certainly welcome you, sir."

Nast looks at Reggie with a raised eyebrow. "Are you pumping the doctor for information my boy?"

Reggie pulls out a chair for the professor. "Please have a seat. We just started to talk Professor. I have not had a chance to grill him about our railroad plans."

"Ah the railroad," Nast smiles. "I had already forgotten that is your main thrust."

De Long watches the banter with interest.

Reggie nods in response to the professor's barb. "Can I get you a glass of wine?"

"Beer is what I thirst for. Do you think this place would have something cold that would taste German?"

Reggie pushes back his chair. "I'll see what they have."

Reggie returns to the table with a dark brown bottle that has metal links attached to the bottle's stopper. Cool beads of sweat form on the outside of the beer.

The professor reaches out for the bottle. "Ah, that certainly looks the part." Pulling the stopper aside the professor puts the bottle to his lips for a long drink. "Not German, but it is cool and the taste is better than the hot beer we have at the camp."

Clive and the doctor engage in a conversation regarding the state of their favorite football clubs. Reggie turns his attention to the professor. "So, from what the doctor tells me, the mines will be in your company's hands soon."

Professor Nast pours the rest of his beer into a glass. "Well it's early days. We do not have an answer from the French as to whether they will agree to sell. The mines are rich and our glass and pottery industry needs the material. The real pluses for me are the cave drawings of a very early civilization. After all, that is why we are here in the first place."

Reggie rises his wine glass. "Here's to your success Professor. If you do buy the company then the railroad will depend on whether you deem it necessary to bring your ore out to the north coast."

"It will not be my company, my boy. The glass company will be the owners. I merely put forth an offer for them. Further negotiations will come from them.

You may not need to stay in this wretched place much longer. We may both be able to leave here soon, I hope."

"That would be welcome news for Clive and me, but I think we still need to finish our mapping before we can go. It would be foolish to leave without a completed map."

Nast leans over to Reggie and in a low voice says, "It would be foolish for you to meddle in this my boy. Please take heed, do not involve yourself further. There are dangers here you do not understand. Please let us dine and forget the rest of this business."

Chapter 48

Claire Fairthorpe can feel her face swelling. She turns her head away from Olaf to run her tongue over her lips. Claire tastes the blood and feels the sting of her split lip. The only thought she has now is how she will kill Olaf to avenge her outrage.

They drive for two days; the only stops are for food and water. Olaf unties Claire's legs so she can relieve herself. She knows she cannot survive without water in the desert. When she returns to the car Olaf reties her legs. He enjoys the control he has over her. As they begin to climb into the mountain range Olaf stops to study his map.

"Where is the expedition camped?"

"I don't know," Claire answers. Without any protection from the sun her face is red, her lips chapped.

Olaf grabs her chin to turn her face toward him. "I will enjoy beating the truth from you if you prefer."

Claire twists away. "All I know is that they are supposed to go to the mines that are west of the fort. If Schulz sees you he will shoot you like the rabid dog you are."

Olaf laughs. "I will deal with Commander Schulz. He and the professor will not survive the desert they both hate. I plan to bury both of them in the sand."

BOBO'S RAID

Claire rubs peeling skin from her nose with her tied hands. "How do you think they will let you even get close to them?"

"Schulz is the only obstacle. The other men will follow my orders. It is only Schulz and the professor who are not party members. We will find the professor's tent and there I will deal with them."

Driving on the only road to the west they come upon the same small village where Doctor De Long has his office. Just outside of the village, Olaf stops. He pulls Claire from the front of the car to bind her arms behind her. After tying a gag over her mouth he shoves her down behind the front seats. Looping rope around the seat frame he secures her to the car then throws a blanket over her.

Olaf drives to the edge of the village and gets out, walking toward some children playing in the dirt. Olaf's voice grows louder trying to make himself understood. The children soon run away from the shrieking giant. A blue-robed Tuareg man, his hand on a long dagger, walks to Olaf.

"Do you know German?" Olaf asks. The Tuareg shakes his head. "French, English?" Again the man shakes his head negatively. "Mien Gott you're all idiots."

Olaf points to the German army cap on his head. The robed man points to the hills behind the village. Olaf follows the man's finger but his view is obstructed by the red clay buildings. Olaf shouts at the man as the Tuareg walks away. "Hey where you going?"

The man beckons Olaf to follow. On the far edge of the village the Tuareg stops and points at the hillside where the tops of some tents can be seen.

Olaf turns back toward the Fiat muttering to himself. "Stupid fools, bathing in their own sweat in that garb must fry their brains."

He returns to the Fiat to remove the blanket, untie the rope and pull Claire up from the back.

"You're going to drive us up to the camp. I'll be in back of you with this pistol pointed at your head. If you say one wrong word it will be your last. Drive through the village and turn up the trail to your left, past the last house. If there's a guard, say you need to see the professor. Now drive."

Olaf gets down behind the seat and pulls the blanket over him.

Claire drives up to the camp trying to think of some way to get away. The camp's tents are on a level patch of ground overlooking the village. There are no guards; the place seems deserted. Claire stops in front of an open tent. "There is no one here."

Olaf cautiously raises his head to look around. "Drive the car around the back of the tents."

Claire drives past the row of tents and turns. Olaf prods Claire with his pistol. "Get the car out of sight. Go park behind those rocks."

Olaf jumps from the back of the Fiat. He opens the driver's side door to yank Claire out. "We'll wait in the professor's tent." He shoves Claire forward with the pistol at her back. Pushing her along he guides her to the larger tent that is the professor's.

Inside the tent, the shade it offers is not much cooler than outside.

The heat bakes the smell of musty canvas into the still air. Olaf pushes Claire to a heavy wooden chair. "This is the professor's prized chair. I've had to pack this thing all over the damned desert. It takes two men to get it in and out of the trucks. Sit down witch. Make yourself comfortable."

Olaf laughs when Claire tries to kick out at him. He ties her arms and legs to the chair before gagging her.

"The only thing that will keep you alive much longer is for you to tell me where the gold is. If there really isn't any gold you better think of something that will make me a rich man. Everyone must be at the mine. That should give you some time to think."

Claire falls asleep in the chair. She wakes to the sound of a truck laboring up the hill to the camp. Olaf peeks out to see who is in the truck, then goes out of the tent.

He returns some time later with a beer and sandwich. Pulling up a camp seat to sit by Claire he opens the beer to take a long drink. Unwrapping the sandwich, he takes a huge bite then sets the sandwich on Claire's knee to drink more of the beer.

"I hope you've had time to think. You always said you were the brains. So what's it going to be, witch?"

Claire tries to talk but shakes her head chewing at the gag.

"Oh you have something to say?" Olaf pulls off the gag.

"There is no gold. If you want a lot of money you need to find the professor."

"Nast? He's not rich. What are you trying to pull?"

"Give me some water you pig and I'll tell you."

Olaf puts the beer bottle to Claire's mouth and tilts it up. She swallows some; the rest runs down her front.

She coughs and twists her head away from the bottle. "Bastard! Look, Bobrowski loves the old man, thinks of him as a father. You get Nast, then tell Bobrowski to get what money you want or you'll kill Nast. Do you think you can manage that?"

"How much does this Bobrowski have?"

"How much do you want? From what I've been told he has a huge fortune. He has houses in England, America, Spain, and the Bahamas. He races very expensive cars all over the world. I would say he is very, very rich. I hope you take him for every penny he has. That would be better than killing him."

"Did he not kiss your ring, witch?"

"Go to hell Olaf. You are as stupid as all the rest. If you do get Bobrowski's money you will still be a stupid donkey."

"I'll be rich and you, my angry little witch, will be dead."

Chapter 49

Professor Nast puts his hand to his mouth to cover a yawn.

"Will you be staying here at the hotel professor?" Reggie asks.

"No, I have to go back to that retched tent with Schulz tonight. After all this time in the desert the tent smells like a goat's insides in the heat of the day. We have other mines to inspect tomorrow so I have to get an early start."

Reggie puts his napkin on the table. "Where is Commander Schulz?"

"He has business at the fort. He was very impressed with the fort. I think he misses that military way of life. All of that saluting and such. Anyway he's going to pick me up here for the ride back to camp. I wanted a good meal away from camp so I came with him. I am delighted to see you. If you are staying we can dine together again."

"Maybe Clive and I could visit you at your camp."

"I would have to clear that with Schulz," Nast snaps. He looks over at Doctor De Long. "You know we are very busy, and Schulz runs a strict camp. Visits are up to him you understand. I am going to take a little walk to the fort, I'll meet Schulz there. Goodnight gentlemen."

Schulz and Nast head back to their camp, the truck's headlight beams dance crazily over the landscape as it rides over rough ground. The cones of illumination show the little berm of rocks marking the road. Going up the hill to the camp the truck bounces off a rut, its lights reach out to be lost in the infinity of the black sky.

Schulz stops the truck at the first tent. "I do not see a guard posted. I'll go see what the men are up to."

Stepping down from the truck Nast says, "I'll be in my tent if you need me Commander. Come by for a beer if you like."

Nast opens the flap of his tent. He first notices that there is light where it should be dark. Then he sees Claire bound in his chair her eyes darting to his right. Nast just starts to turn his head when an arm goes around his neck to lift him from the ground. His hands go to the arm to pull it away. The struggle is brief, blackness pours into Nast's brain as he goes limp.

"If you've killed him, you stupid fool, your fortune is lost."

Olaf drops the professor to slap Claire. Her head snaps back from the blow.

"You will not live through the night if you call me stupid again."

Olaf pulls the gag around Claire's head tight. He picks up Nast and throws him on a cot like a rag doll.

To Claire he says, "Stay very still, you filthy cow. Schulz will be here soon."

Olaf takes his heavy bolt action rifle with him to keep watch at the tent's entrance.

A half hour passes before Olaf moves quickly to the shadows, picking up his rifle by the barrel. Schulz pushes past the tent flap. He immediately sees Claire and goes to her to bend down and untie her legs. Olaf creeps forward with the rifle posed above his head. Schulz with some sixth sense stops untying Claire to turn around.

Olaf brings the rifle down with all his might. The butt of the rifle smashes into the commander's head with so much force blood and brain matter spray out. Claire shakes violently in the chair; blood and clots of matter run down her face. What is left of the commander's ruined head is buried between her legs.

Olaf, breathing hard, laughs hysterically. "I have wanted to do that for ages."

He grabs Schulz's legs to pull him from the tent. The body leaves a furrow of blood in the sand and dirt.

When Olaf returns to the tent he stands over Nast who is snoring softly. "Sleep well little man." He loops a rope over Nast and around the cot.

Claire rocks her chair trying get Olaf's attention.

"Sit still, witch. If you knock that chair over you won't get up. I have to get one of my men to take a message to your friend Bobrowski. Keep your buttons on, you can wait until I return."

Reggie wakes in his hotel room to a still cool morning; he yawns and stretches. Heading to the bathroom he finds an envelope on the floor that was pushed under his door. Tearing the envelope open he reads the words printed with a pencil in large childlike block letters. With some difficulty Reggie discerns the message to mean that someone is holding the professor for ransom. They want 100,000.00 pounds sterling for his safe return.

The bottom of the note reads, "Commander Schulz is killed and Nast will be next. You will to be contacted in two days. Have the money."

Reggie goes to Clive's room. When Clive opens his door Reggie shows him the note. "Is this real? Clive exclaims. "Who would kidnap Nast and how would they think you would pay the ransom?"

Reggie paces the room. "It has to be someone at the camp. The only people I can think of that make sense are Claire or Olaf. Maybe they're both in on it. Saddle up; we need to go up to our lookout post and see if we can find out what goes on at the camp."

High above the camp both men are on their bellies sweating in the heat. They have their binoculars trained on the German camp going over every square foot.

Clive nudges Reggie. "Look at the big tent on the south end of the camp. See the trail on the ground in front of the tent's entrance?"

Reggie focuses in on the ground in front of the tent. "Good eye Jonesy. That looks like something bloody was dragged out of the tent."

The tent's entrance flap opens. A man pushes a woman with her hands bound from the tent. The woman stumbles, her legs don't seem to want to carry her weight. The man kicks her to the ground then yanks her to her feet and pushes her forward.

"It's Claire and Olaf," Reggie whispers.

"Where's he taking her? Do you think they can hear us?"

"No probably not," Reggie answers. "I don't know if the air carries our voices or not. They have guards posted but no one with binoculars that I've seen. I think he's taking her to the latrine."

BOBO'S RAID

Clive says, "Claire looked a mess. I almost feel sorry for her."

Reggie lifts the binoculars to his eyes. "They're coming back."

Olaf pushes Claire along to the tent. After a few minutes he emerges to walk to another tent. He comes back with a rake to cover the blood on the trail in front of the tent he took Claire in. He works the rake back and forth spreading dirt and sand, then throws the rake behind the tent.

He reenters the tent and a few minutes later leads the professor out down the same way he took Claire.

"Okay Jonesy, there's no doubt he has Nast. Take the Citroën back to the fort and get help. I don't want the soldiers bursting in. Tell them they have to come in quietly. If they come in guns blazing, Olaf will probably kill the professor and Claire."

"What are you going to do, Reg? You're not thinking of going it alone are you?"

"No, I want to make sure he doesn't take them someplace else. If he moves them, we need to know where. Get going now; it may take hours before you can get back with help."

Time weighs heavily on Reggie. The longer he waits the more he thinks of the professor being hurt or killed when Clive returns with the French Legionnaires. He is sure Olaf won't give up without a fight. Knowing the legionnaires will not hesitate to storm the camp, Reggie fears Olaf will kill Professor Nast.

As more time drags by, Reggie's fears deepen. He crawls back behind the hilltop to smoke a cigarette. Lighting another cigarette his anxiety gets the best of him. He crushes out the cigarette and crawls back to the hilltop. Watching the camp through his binoculars Reggie sees only two guards. Both guards stay at opposite ends of the camp smoking cigarettes in the shade.

Reggie climbs down the mountain out of sight of the camp. Once down in the valley he climbs up a foothill on the backside of the camp. There are outcrops of large rock to conceal him from anyone in the camp. Only yards away from the professor's tent now, he stops to listen for any sounds of movement.

The last ten yards are without any cover. He does not want to raise any dust to give him away. Crouched down, his back tensed, he walks toward the tent. He can feel rifles pointed at him from every angle. Hairs on the back of his neck bristle. At last next to the tent, he lies prone to give the smallest profile and listens for movement in the tent.

There is only silence in the professor's tent. He can hear voices from one of the other tents. Reggie works one of the steel tent pegs that are hammered into the ground. Pulling the heavy steel peg back and forth he loosens it from the ground and out of the tent's grommet. Sweat rolls down his forehead stinging his eyes. The tent's pegs are placed about two feet apart. He needs to get two more out to be able to get under the tent. Working another peg from the ground he stops dead when hears Olaf's voice from inside the tent.

Olaf talks to the professor, "I just wanted to make sure you are comfortable Professor. I'm off for a drink with my men, don't wait up for me." Olaf laughs as he leaves the tent.

Reggie waits a few minutes, the sun beating down, his shirt soaked with sweat. With some renewed resolve he pulls the peg up, then the next one. Lifting the edge of the tent slowly, he looks into the interior of the tent. His eyes take time to adjust from the harsh sunlight to the darker interior.

Reggie can see he is near the professor's cot. Rolling under the canvas he snakes under the cot then turns on his back to get a knife from his pocket. Rising up between the side of the tent and the cot he reaches out to cover the professor's mouth with his hand. Nast jerks his head up his eyes wide. Reggie nods and pats Nast's arm before bringing his finger to his mouth to signal quiet.

With Nast calmed, Reggie saws at the ropes that bind the man. Nast swings his legs over the edge of the cot to crouch by Reggie. Nast puts his face close to Reggie to whisper, "He has Claire tied to a chair. Can you get her out?"

"I'll come back for her once you're safe," Reggie whispers. "We need to go; follow me. Reggie goes under the canvas then turns to help the professor out. Bent over holding the canvas up, Reggie receives a tremendous blow on his back. He is yanked to his feet and struck hard on his face. Knocked to the ground he looks up into the face of a madman.

Reggie scrambles to get to his feet and lashes out with a good right uppercut that snaps the gorilla's head back. Olaf grins maniacally, punching Reggie on the jaw. Grabbing Reggie's shirt he throws him to the ground, then pounces to straddle Reggie's chest. Olaf's huge hands tighten around the downed man's throat. Reggie's vision blurs as he struggles to stay alive.

Olaf grunts, his hands lose their grip on Reggie's throat as he falls forward. Reggie struggles to push Olaf off him. Nast looks down on Olaf, a tent peg in his hand. "Did I kill him? I hit him on the head as hard as I could."

Reggie breathing hard grabs Nast arm. "I think you just knocked him out. Let's get out of here while we can."

Nast drops the tent peg to follow Reggie.

Chapter 50

Climbing back up the mountain Reggie supports Nast who is running on empty, his strength sapped. Clive is there to help the two men to the summit. "I knew you were going to do something foolish old man."

Small arms fire erupts from the camp. Reggie, still panting, picks up his binoculars to focus on the action below. Both of the German guards are down. French soldiers in their distinctive white caps have surrounded the camp. The rifle fire is sporadic.

Olaf comes to, his head splitting with pain. Slowly he gets to his feet. As he stands, his head pounding, it takes a moment for him to realize what has happened. Gently probing the back of his head, his hand comes away bloody. Olaf's face clouds with rage.

Crawling under the tent, the first thing Olaf focuses on is Claire still tied to the chair. Her mouth is still gagged but her eyes smile back at Olaf. She is overjoyed to see his failure. Olaf's huge hands ball in fists. He goes behind Claire's heavy chair and kicks it over. Claire's head hits the ground hard. Olaf puts his boot on the back of the chair forcing her head deeper into the sand. He smiles down at Claire. "Breathe sand, you witch."

When the rifle fire erupts closer, Olaf scrambles to find his Luger pistol. Peeping out of the tent he sees a legionnaire. He slips the pistol down the back of his shirt collar. Smiling to himself he mutters, "I'll kill a few of these stupid frog fools, get in the truck and be gone before any of them know what hit them."

Olaf comes out of the tent with his hands locked behind his head. He walks toward the legionnaire in submission. Suddenly the German has a pistol in his hand aimed at the Frenchman. Olaf shoots first, the legionnaire goes down. A legionnaire, crouched by one of the trucks unseen by Olaf, snaps a shot off at the German. The bullet burns a furrow across his stomach. Olaf staggers backward, then turns to run hunched over back into the professor's tent.

Bullets follow him ripping through the tent. Going back under the rear of the tent Olaf races for the Fiat parked behind the rocks. The old car coughs to life; Olaf jams it into gear to roar out behind the row of tents. At the end of the row Olaf has to slow to turn hard left. He hopes to catch the soldiers by surprise. Bursting out to the road Olaf meets a fusillade of French lead.

Olaf screams like a banshee as bullets tear through his body. The Fiat clips the back of one of the trucks, skids sideways, then digs in. Barrel rolling down the hill, the Fiat spits out Olaf's body, rolls over it, and continues down the hill.

The French soldiers rush the tents pulling open the flaps and firing on whatever they find inside.

Reggie lowers his binoculars and speaks to Clive. "That is just what I was afraid of. I could just see the professor being shot either by Olaf or the legionnaires before anyone would realize he was not an enemy."

Reggie turns around to see the professor sitting out of the sun by the Citroën, his head in his hands.

Reggie squeezes Nast's shoulder. "Don't feel bad professor. You didn't kill Olaf. He just tried to shoot it out with the legionnaires and practically killed himself."

Nast sits up; his back straightens as if a weight has been removed. "I could not let him kill you my boy, but I am very relieved that I did not kill him."

Reggie grins at the professor and calls to Clive, "Let's get back to the hotel and pick up our things. We better hustle the professor away. I think the legionnaires will want to hold someone accountable for this."

Epilogue

Clive and Reggie marvel at just how green the English countryside looks. The months in the desert will never be forgotten, but the past adventure makes being home with their wives even sweeter than before.

They drove the professor to In Salah, Clive making reports to London on the way. The PM promised to try and make amends with the Algerian French. Nast used the Citroën's radio to make his report and to arrange for an airplane meet them.

Once they reached In Salah, Reggie radioed Marshal Balbo with directions to pick up the Citroën.

In London Clive and Reggie meet with the Prime Minister. After a short wait at number 10 Downing Street the PM greets them warmly.

"Gentlemen, you have done your country a great service. The intelligence community had not recognized the ultimate goal of the German's exploration. I can not go into the nature of what it all means. What I can say is that I am very grateful for your work."

Walking out into the cool London air Clive turns to Reggie, "What's that all mean Reg?"

"I think, my friend, the Jerrys have found another use for uranium, and it's not just for coloring glass."

After resting up a few days, Clive and Reggie are in the garage of Reggie's country house.

"I say, old cock, do we start a new Citroën or plan the next race?"

Alexandra and Fay come into the garage with trays of tea and biscuits.

Smiling mischievously Ally says, "We say, old cocks, we plan a grand shopping trip in New York while visiting my parents."

Clive and Reggie look at each other in dismay. "Oh my god," Clive groans.

Thank you for reading Bobo's Raid. I hope you enjoyed reading it as much as I enjoyed writing it.

The website where you bought your book should have a review option. I really appreciate reviews. They are very helpful to me because I'm interested in learning what you enjoy reading so I can continue to make my books fun for you to read. And book reviews are the way book sellers rank the books in their sales lists. The more reviews we get, the higher we rank, and the easier it is to find us in the book lists.

Reviewing can be as easy as clicking stars or as detailed as you would like to make your comments. In any case I really appreciate your interest in my work.

Connect with me online

**Mike Downs Mysteries website:
http://www.mikedownsmysteries.com
Facebook: Mike Downs, and Mike Downs Mysteries
Twitter: #MikeDownsAuthor
Goodreads: Mike Downs**

About the Author

I started racing for Group 44, the factory Triumph sports car team on the East coast. After wining a national championship I moved to California to race the new Titan Formula Ford for the West Coast distributor.

I raced for forty years in TransAm, IMSA,Formula Atlantic, and FIA endurance races. I drove factory cars for Triumph, Porsche, Datsun, and Titan. I won the last championship with a sports car I designed and built at my company, Downs Engineering. Downs Engineering builds race cars, specialty cars, and Hayabusa racing engines. For more information ,please visit our website at http://www.downsengineering.com.

All my racing reinforced my respect and admiration for the racing pioneers that have gone before. The drivers, team owners, car builders, and fabricators have inspired my stories.

I live in Northern California with my lovely wife Kathy.

Made in the USA
Charleston, SC
17 January 2014